D0206979

COMMANDO DAD:
NEW RECRUITS

COMMANDO DAD:
NEW RECRUITS

A Guide to Pregnancy and Birth
for Dads-to-Be

Neil Sinclair

CHRONICLE BOOKS

SAN FRANCISCO

I would like to dedicate this book to my own unit.

To my wife, Tara: although our parenting adventures were always unplanned, they're still brilliant because we're having them together.

To Sam, Jude, and Liberty: I love you very much and hope that you use the lessons we learned together when you bring your own troopers into this world.

First published in the United States of America in 2015 by Chronicle Books LLC.
First published in the United Kingdom as *Commando Dad: Raw Recruits* in 2014 by Yellow Kite, an imprint of Hodder & Stoughton.

Text copyright © 2014 by Neil Sinclair and Tara Sinclair.
Illustrations copyright © 2014 by Matt Smith.

Library of Congress Cataloging-in-Publication Data available.

ISBN 978-1-4521-4552-5

Manufactured in China

FSC www.fsc.org — MIX Paper from responsible sources FSC™ C016973

Designed by Ben Kither

The information in this book should not be treated as a substitute for qualified medical advice. Always consult a medical practitioner. Neither the author nor the publisher can be held responsible for any loss or claim arising out of the use, or misuse, of the suggestions made or the failure to take medical advice.

10 9 8 7 6 5 4 3 2 1

Chronicle Books LLC
680 Second Street
San Francisco, California 94107
www.chroniclebooks.com

Disclaimer

I have written this book based on my own experiences. Where I reference the health and safety of your CO or your BTs, I have had the text reviewed and approved by health care professionals to ensure that the information is accurate and in line with current thinking and practice at the time of publication. However, the publisher, author, and experts disclaim any liability from any injury that may result from the use, proper or improper, of the information contained in this book. Guidance and guidelines on pregnancy and childbirth change constantly, and *Commando Dad: New Recruits* should not be considered a substitute for the advice of your health care professional or your own common sense.

About the Author

I'm an ex-Royal Engineer commando, and in my six years of service, I served 3 tours in Norway, a tour in the jungles of Belize, and 6 months in the mountains of Iraq as part of Operation Desert Storm. I cleared mines, tracked drug barons through the jungle, and skied across crevasse-riddled ice fields. But none of this prepared me for my most challenging mission: for the past 11 years I have been a stay-at-home dad to my three troopers: Sam, Jude, and Liberty.

I used all of my experiences to write a book for new dads called *Commando Dad: A Basic Training Manual for the First Three Years of Fatherhood*. It's a clear, concise manual offering straightforward advice on the practical skills needed to be an effective dad. It's the parenting equivalent of *Basic Battle Skills*, the no-nonsense field training guide issued to all soldiers in the British Army. It struck a chord with a lot of new dads. However, on the Commando Dad website forums there are a lot of dads-to-be looking for information and support, and this gave me the inspiration to write *Commando Dad: New Recruits*. This is the book I wish I'd been issued with when I found out I was going to be a new dad. It will give you everything you need to know for the whole 266 days. And counting.

CONTENTS

Foreword   8

Introduction   10

1: New Recruits: 266 Days and Counting   14

2: Actions on Appointments   36

3: Fit for Fatherhood   56

4: Call the Doctor   74

5: Report to the Stores: Essential Equipment that You Need to Acquire   84

6: Deployment Day   98

7: What Happens Next   118

8: When Things Don't Go as Planned   134

9: Special Ops: When Your Experience Is Different from the Norm   152

10: Mission Debrief   166

Glossary: Breaking the Code   170

Index   185

Acknowledgments   191

Foreword

In today's society, dads are actively encouraged to bond with their babies while they are still in the womb and to be at the birth, acting as birth companions and offering support and encouragement to their partners throughout labor. But where do they get the skills to do this? Where do they have the opportunity to find out about what is going to happen to their partner and therefore how they can be most effective? How do they know what to expect when they see their partner in pain, or what to do when they bring their baby home from the hospital?

While there is an overwhelming amount of information on pregnancy and labor that can be accessed through books, forums, and the media, the majority is aimed at moms, or couples in general, not specifically at dads. As someone who works with fathers, I am continually aware of the need to make it relevant for them, to ensure that they are receiving the information that they need and that they have the opportunity to discuss the things that concern *them*.

I am therefore delighted that Commando Dad has used his winning formula of combining concise information, real-life experience, illustrations, and summaries to cover all the essential topics related to pregnancy, birth, and those first few weeks in this outstanding book. The number of subjects that he has managed to cover, and in such detail, ensures that this is one book no dad can afford to be without.

Those who work with dads know that if couples have the opportunity to make informed choices throughout pregnancy and during birth, they are better able to adjust to becoming parents. Commando Dad has provided all the essential information dads (and moms) need to make those choices.

Dads, I recommend you use the chapters in this book as the basis for discussions with your partner about the choices that are available to you as a couple: for example, where do you want your baby to be born? To deliberate over the types of pain management available and to know in advance of deployment day what your partner might want—or not want! To think and then discuss together how your lives are going to change as individuals and as a couple, and what you might feel on meeting your baby for the first time.

And with only 266 days to prepare for this life-changing experience, there is not a moment to lose. I recommend you start reading immediately!

New Recruits is simply the most essential toolkit for all dads-to-be, whether they are expecting their first or third baby.

Kate Bedding
BA (Hons), M.Res, PGDip, PGCE,
Diploma Postnatal Facilitation NCT,
Diploma Antenatal Education NCT,
PhD student (Midwifery—UCLAN)

Introduction

TO ALL DADS-TO-BE (henceforth known as Commando Dads):
This book has been written for YOU.

When I first found out that I was going to be a dad, I felt a lot of emotions, the main one of which was definitely fear. We weren't trying to start a family—we hadn't even been thinking about it. I'd been married only 18 months. None of my friends were dads. I'd never even held a baby. And yet in less than 266 days, I was going to be a dad.

Gentlemen, I don't use the word "fear" lightly. As a commando I experienced truly frightening situations. I soon realized that I didn't fear being a dad—that was now inevitable—rather, I feared the unknown.

I wanted to get educated in the basics as fast as the situation demanded. I wanted to know what was going to physically happen to my wife (moms-to-be are henceforth known as COs or Commanding Officers); I wanted to know what I could do to help; I wanted to know the practicalities of pregnancy—appointments and scans and classes; I wanted to know about labor.

The books that were available focused exclusively on this kind of mental preparation via huge amounts of detailed information. Although the content was essential, there was so much of it that it was overwhelming—I suffered sensory overload. Also, now that I have been through pregnancy and childbirth with my CO, I know that mental preparation is only part of the story. Men also need to be physically and emotionally prepared.

The manual that you are holding in your hands will provide you with clear and concise guidance on what to expect, from the moment you find out you're going to be a dad until the moment your baby trooper (BT) deploys. It will help to mentally, physically, and emotionally prepare you for fatherhood, but it will not saturation bomb you with information.

Although your CO alone is facing the intense demands of pregnancy and childbirth, do not feel you have no place. That would be to fundamentally misunderstand your role as a dad. It starts now. You need to be essential backup support to your CO—she needs you. You need to provide physical support when she is tired, emotional support when she is feeling down, and mental support when she is perhaps overwhelmed or fearful. This will help pave the way for a new little life that you have helped to create. What you do from this point forward really counts. This book will help.

HOW TO USE *COMMANDO DAD: NEW RECRUITS*

Commando Dad: New Recruits is your essential coursebook for 9 months. It supports your active participation in the pregnancy and childbirth process. Keep it close and refer to it often.

The book is supported by the Commando Dad website, where you will find extra resources, helpful "how to" videos, and forums where dads can provide you with help, support, and advice on every question you need to ask. There is no such thing as a stupid question. As you gain skills, experience, and confidence, I would ask that you remain on the forums to help other Commando Dads as they do their bit to swell the ranks. Please log on to find out what's available: www.commandodad.com.

Throughout *Commando Dad: New Recruits* I use the following terms:

- ★ **CO:** your Commanding Officer—the person in charge—that is, the mom-to-be
- ★ **BT:** your baby trooper

I have also included quotes from new dads, in the "Advice from the Front Line" sections. All of these dads use the Commando Dad forums, and they responded to a call for action to help dads-to-be just like you.

The journey that you are now on is an inherently emotional one. You will probably already know this because of how you felt when you found out that you were going to be a dad. For me, the main response was fear, but other new dads have told me they've felt anguish, awe, contentment, excitement, gratitude, joy, panic, relief, shock, wonder, and worry. And they're just the ones I've spoken to. Throughout pregnancy, there are significant milestones that may trigger huge emotional responses, and to make you aware of these, I have created "Emotion Alerts" throughout the book. I am not telling you what emotions to feel and when. You may find that you feel very emotional throughout the whole nine months or that you feel very little emotion until your BT deploys (is born). There is no right or wrong way to be feeling.

Where I want to draw your attention to something that may require urgent medical assistance, I have used the heading "Call the Doctor." For things that may require medical assistance, I have used the heading "Doctor: Stand By." For more information about conditions that require urgent medical attention, and pregnancy complications, see *Chapter 4: Call the Doctor.*

Throughout the book I refer to you and your CO going to the hospital to give birth. This is because it is the most common place for births to happen. If you and your CO choose to use a birthing center, a home birth, or an alternative, a lot of the information in the book is still relevant to you. Please also see *Chapter 9: Special Ops.*

RECAP AND REFRESH

I have worked hard to ensure that I cover a lot of information in this book, and at the end of every chapter I have included a brief summary of the main topics covered and signposted where you can find other information that may be relevant to you.

COMMANDO DAD GOLDEN RULES

There are 5 golden rules that will stand you in good stead for the next 266 days. They will also lay the foundations for the elite standards you will be working toward and operating at, as a new dad:

1. A Commando Dad knows that preparation and planning prevent poor parental performance. Get ready. Now. Get as much information as you can; if there is anything you don't understand, ask.
2. A Commando Dad knows when to ask for and accept help—for both himself and his CO.
3. A Commando Dad is a problem solver. In any given situation he will improvise, adapt, and overcome.
4. A Commando Dad keeps calm under pressure.
5. A Commando Dad takes care of his unit with all the means at his disposal.

NEW RECRUITS

266 Days and Counting

THE BRIEF

Fewer than 266 days separate you from fatherhood. A period of massive physical—and potentially emotional—change lies ahead for your CO as your BT is created, grows, and develops. Arm yourself now with essential information about the changes that lie ahead. Planning and preparation prevent poor parental performance.

THE OBJECTIVE

Every BT develops differently, and no two COs experience pregnancy in the same way. But by the end of this chapter you will have an overview of the physical changes that your CO will undergo over the next 9 months—from conception to deployment. You will understand how the growth of your BT impacts her body and will have an overview of your BT's development.

ADVICE FROM THE FRONT LINE

"I was a hands-on dad from day one. It was all about looking after the wife and making sure she had everything she needed—from food to sleep. It was all about her and the unborn! Some fellas are not prepared for this or the ups and downs (which happen a lot), but as we worked as a team we were able to manage this and it made us stronger."
PAUL HOPE

EMOTION ALERT

Your fatherhood journey starts here. While it is not going to be a physical one—at least not for the next 9 months—be aware that it may be an emotional one. When you find out that you're going to be a dad, you can't help but analyze your experiences with your own dad and start drawing conclusions. Maybe you didn't have a father figure in your life and wonder if that will affect your ability to be a good dad; maybe you had a fantastic dad and wonder if you will ever be able to be as good as he was with your own troopers; maybe your dad's fathering skills left a lot to be desired and you're worried that you may make the same mistakes. While I can't speak to these maybes, I can tell you a definite: the only person who has any control over what kind of dad you'll be is you. So decide to be the best dad you can be. This starts by supporting your CO now.

She may be feeling anxious about becoming a parent, but she also has soaring pregnancy hormones to deal with. These will have physical and emotional effects. Anticipate that she may have mood swings, especially in the early days. You may find that you are bearing the brunt of these rapidly changing emotions, but try not to take it personally. Your CO is on an emotional rollercoaster. Be there and reassure her that everything is OK. Mood swings should start to stabilize after around 12 weeks.

TERMS USED IN THE MONTH-BY-MONTH BREAKDOWN

TRIMESTERS
Your CO's pregnancy is split into 3 parts, or trimesters. Different practitioners may use different markers to determine the start and end dates of each trimester. The most common division is as follows:
- ★ **First trimester:** 2–13 weeks
  - » Your CO is considered to be 2 weeks into her pregnancy when fertilization occurs. As it is impossible to predict the moment of conception, it is counted from a date that is known; that is, the start of her last period.
- ★ **Second trimester:** 14–26 weeks
- ★ **Third trimester:** 27–40 weeks

SYMPTOMS
In this chapter I detail some possible symptoms that your CO may experience throughout her pregnancy. The month I have put them in indicates when this symptom may first appear. In reality she may experience none of these symptoms, or experience them all throughout her entire pregnancy, or experience them at different times. Every pregnancy is different.

WEIGHT GAIN
The average weight gain for a CO over the course of a pregnancy is 25–35 lb/11–16 kg, broken down as follows:
- ★ BT: 8 lb/3.6 kg
- ★ Placenta: 2–3 lb/1–1.4 kg
- ★ Amniotic fluid: 2–3 lb/1–1.4 kg
- ★ Breast tissue: 2–3 lb/1–1.4 kg
- ★ Blood supply: 4 lb/2 kg
- ★ Stored fat for delivery and breastfeeding: 5–9 lb/2.2–4 kg
- ★ Larger uterus: 2–5 lb/1–2.2 kg

But weight gain will be dependent on a number of factors, including your CO's body shape and weight going into pregnancy. Your CO will need to speak to her doctor or midwife, who can provide tailored advice about her weight gain. For this reason, I haven't included any weight gain information in the tables that follow. See *Chapter 3: Fit for Fatherhood* for advice on healthy eating during pregnancy to ensure that you and your CO—and your BT—have the nourishment you need.

ADVICE FROM
THE FRONT LINE

"The CO will be going through a huge number of changes—physically and emotionally—so be there to support her, reassure her, and tell her that everything will be all right."

CALUM BEATT

MONTH 1 (weeks 2–4)

FIRST TRIMESTER
Life begins
Your BT

- ★ Size: a pinhead by month end.
- ★ Your BT is a ball of cells that is dividing into 3 layers that will later form organs and tissues.
- ★ The placenta is functioning, but will continue to develop and perform more complex tasks.

Your CO

Possible physical changes

None

Possible symptoms | **Possible causes**

Possible symptoms	Possible causes
Missed or abnormal period	A shorter or lighter "period" may actually be caused by a fertilized egg burrowing into the lining of her uterus.
Morning sickness (despite the misleading name, it can last all day)	No definitive answer, but it is thought that fluctuating pregnancy hormones are the culprit.

DOCTOR: STAND BY

Call your medical support team if your CO's morning sickness never goes away or if she is vomiting several times a day, loses weight, and feels dizzy and faint. This could be a condition called hyperemesis gravidarum, which requires medical assistance.

MONTH 2 (weeks 5–8)

FIRST TRIMESTER
Critical development commences
Your BT

★ Size: pinhead to 0.5 in/1.3 cm.
★ The following begin to form:
  » The digestive tract—stomach and intestines.
  » The sensory organs—eyes, ears, tongue, transparent skin, and nose.
  » The neural tube—brain, spinal cord, and other nerve tissue.

- » The respiratory system—lungs.
- » The circulatory system—blood and heart, which begins to beat.
- » Limb buds—which will eventually become arms, together with distinguishable feet and hands.
- » Tooth buds and palate.
- » Muscle and bone.

 COMMANDO DAD TOP TIP
You and your CO are in this together. If you're not already, you both need to adopt a healthy lifestyle: eating well, no drinking, and no smoking. Getting fit or maintaining fitness levels is also good for both of you. See *Chapter 3: Fit for Fatherhood* for more information.

ADVICE FROM THE FRONT LINE

"When it comes to the CO, do not complain about anything. Nothing you are experiencing, either physically or emotionally, comes close to pregnancy. If you ever forget this, you will be reminded in short order."
JOHN ALLEN

Your CO

Possible physical changes	Possible causes
Thickening waistline	Your CO's uterus is growing in size.
Larger breasts	Preparation for breastfeeding (see below).
Faster-growing, thicker hair than usual	Thought to occur because of pregnancy hormones.

Possible symptoms	Possible causes
Increased fatigue	Your CO's body is working overtime to create your BT. Soaring progesterone levels can make her sleepy, while lower blood sugar levels, lower blood pressure, and increased blood production can increase the feelings of tiredness.
Dizziness	Lower blood pressure might cause dizziness or light-headedness, but also hunger or fatigue.
Sensitive breasts	Fluctuating hormones— estrogen and progesterone—and growth of the breasts to prepare for breastfeeding. The fat layer in them thickens, milk glands multiply, and blood flow increases.
Increased urination, and sometimes leaking urine when sneezing, coughing, or laughing	Blood volume is increased, so kidneys are working harder. As the pregnancy progresses, the growing uterus will increasingly put pressure on the bladder.
Stuffy or runny nose	Thought to occur because pregnancy hormones, specifically estrogen, affect the mucous membranes in your CO's nose.
Food cravings and/or aversions Heightened sense of smell	Not conclusive, but extreme hormonal changes are thought to have a huge impact on taste and smell.
Mood swings	Fluctuating hormone levels and anxiety caused by going through an intense period of change.

Continues

Possible symptoms	Possible causes
Heartburn **Constipation**	Progesterone relaxing the muscle that keeps food in the stomach (the gastroesophageal sphincter) and/or food staying in your CO's stomach longer. This gives the food more time to be absorbed into her bloodstream, maximizing the nutrition that your BT can take from it.

 COMMANDO DAD TOP TIP

Increased urination may make your CO inclined to drink less. However, she'll need to keep hydrated, but she should avoid diuretics like tea or coffee, which will just exacerbate the problem. Water is a great choice.

ADVICE FROM THE FRONT LINE

"In terms of backup support, just be there for your CO and listen. Her body is going through massive changes—yours is not!"
SAM WINTERSON

MONTH 3 (weeks 9–13)

FIRST TRIMESTER
BT fully forms—fine-tuning of physiology begins
Your BT

★ Size: 0.7–2.6 in/1.8–6.7 cm from crown (top) of head to bottom.
★ Twelve weeks after your CO's last period, your BT is fully formed, with organs, muscles, limbs, and bones in place; they just need to grow and mature.
★ The following are now formed:
  » Arms.
  » Hands.

» Feet and toes.
» Skin—but it is still transparent.
» Vital organs—heart, liver, kidneys, intestines, brain, and lungs—are functional.
» The circulatory and urinary systems are formed and now performing more complex tasks, and the liver produces bile and red blood cells.
» Placenta.

★ The following begin to form:
» Face.
» Genitals. Sex can't be determined yet, although sex organs are well developed.
» Neurological connections in the brain (synapses).

★ BT becomes active: swallowing fluid, opening and closing hands, kicking limbs. These movements can be detected by ultrasound.

Your CO

Possible physical changes	Possible causes
Linea nigra—a brown line of pigmentation between the belly button and the pubic bone—may appear (sometimes it may extend farther up the abdomen)	Pregnancy hormones cause a darkening of the skin. It will fade after the birth.
Hair, fingernails, and toenails are growing faster	Pregnancy hormones and multivitamins.
Oily skin and/or acne	Pregnancy hormones causing increased blood flow and oil production (which causes the pregnancy "glow").

Possible symptoms	Possible causes
Problems sleeping	A number of reasons: more vivid dreams, discomfort of pregnancy symptoms, and possible anxiety about the pregnancy.

MONTH 4 (weeks 14–17)

SECOND TRIMESTER
Rapid growth begins
Your BT

★ Size: 3.15–4.3 in/8–11 cm from crown of head to bottom.

★ The following are now formed:

» Facial features: your BT can squint, frown, grimace, yawn, and make faces.

» Eyelids, nails, and hair.

» Fingers and unique fingerprints; your BT may suck their thumb.

» Toes.

» Lungs—your BT is now inhaling and exhaling the amniotic fluid they're immersed in.

» Circulatory and urinary systems.

» Genitals. Sex can now be determined with an ultrasound scan.

★ Your BT's skeleton continues to form—it's mostly pliable tissue, cartilage, but it will gradually harden throughout pregnancy, apart from the head, which will need to remain pliable so that it can pass through your CO's birth canal during labor.

★ Teeth and bones become denser.

★ The following begin to form:

» Hair on head, eyebrows, and eyelashes.

» Fat, which will help your BT's heat production and metabolism.

» Sweat glands.

Your CO

Possible physical changes	Possible causes
A more obvious baby bump	A growing uterus that can no longer be hidden. Skin, muscle, and ligaments begin to stretch.

Possible symptoms	Possible causes
Fluttering movements inside ("quickening")	Your CO can feel your BT moving.
Less frequent urination	Your CO's uterus is shifting.
Nosebleeds and/or more noticeable veins	Your CO's blood volume is increasing.
Increased energy and appetite	The side effects that your CO experienced in the first trimester may start to subside.
Heartburn	Thought to occur because the pregnancy hormone progesterone (whch relaxes the muscles of your CO's uterus) may relax the valve that separates her esophagus from her stomach. Later in the pregnancy, heartburn will be caused by a large uterus pushing your CO's stomach and intestines upward.

MONTH 5 (weeks 18–21)

SECOND TRIMESTER
Midway: your BT is very active
Your BT

★ Size: 4.7 in/12 cm from crown of head to rump and 10.6 in/27 cm from head to heel. From around 20 weeks your BT's legs are no longer tightly curled up, making it possible to measure from head to heel.

★ The following are now formed:
  » Reflexes: your BT would suck if their lips were stroked; they can swallow and get hiccups (silent, though, as there's no air in their throat).

★ The following continue to form:
  » The nerve cells serving each of the senses—taste, smell, hearing, seeing, and touch—are developing in their specialized areas of the brain.
  » Taste: your BT's taste buds are beginning to develop, and they can distinguish sweet from bitter tastes.
  » Hearing: your BT can now hear your CO's voice (and perhaps yours), her heart, and her stomach rumbling and growling, as well as sounds outside her body. One of the reasons your BT will find your saying "shh" so calming when the BT deploys is because it reminds them of the sound of your CO's blood pumping through her veins.
  » Seeing: your BT's retinas are sensitive to light.
  » Skin (still transparent). Blood vessels are visible through it.
  » Meconium forms from materials ingested in the uterus. It will appear in their diaper after birth and for the first 2–3 days as a very sticky, dark green poop.

★ The following begin to form:
  » Vernix caseosa, a waxy substance that protects your BT's skin from amniotic fluid and keeps it supple.

Your CO

Possible physical changes	Possible causes
Obviously pregnant	
No waist	Your CO's uterus moves up out of her pelvis.
Tiny red marks on the face, shoulders, and arms	Dilated blood vessels.

Possible symptoms	Possible causes
Lower abdominal aches and pains	Physical changes as the uterus continues to grow.
Increased sweating	Increased activity in the thyroid gland.

MONTH 6 (weeks 22–26)

SECOND TRIMESTER
Intense brain development
Your BT

★ Size: 11–14.2 in/28–36 cm from crown of head to heel.

★ The following are now formed:

» Eyes, which are now open, though they don't have any color yet.

» Taste buds.

★ The following continue to form:

» Fat.

» The pancreas—essential to producing hormones.

» Brain.

» Patterns of sleeping and waking.

★ The following begin to form:

  » Lanugo, a very fine, soft hair that covers your BT's paper-thin skin. Your BT will begin to shed this shortly before birth.

Your CO

Possible physical changes	Possible causes
Belly button pops out	Your CO's expanding uterus pushes her abdomen forward.
Stretch marks on abdomen, buttocks, breasts, and thighs	Rapid growth and stretching of your CO's skin.
Increased vaginal discharge	Your CO's body increases discharge to help prevent infection.

Possible symptoms	Possible causes
Changes to eyes: dry, sore, red, or watery	Sometimes called "dry eye syndrome"—thought to occur because of a drop in your CO's male hormones.
Achy, burning, or tingly fingers, wrists, and hands	Carpal tunnel syndrome: fluid retention and swelling can increase the pressure in the carpal tunnel (or passageway) in your CO's wrist, pinching the nerve that runs through it.
Feeling/being off balance	Your CO's center of gravity has now shifted.
Itchy skin	Rapid growth and stretching of your CO's skin.

DOCTOR: STAND BY

Call your medical support team if your CO has vaginal discharge that is discolored or smells strange or if she feels itchy. She may have an infection. Also call your medical support team if her hands, feet, and abdomen are increasingly itchy, as this may be a sign of cholestasis.

MONTH 7 (weeks 27–30)

THIRD TRIMESTER

Central nervous system and organs mature

Your BT

★ Size: 14.2–15.7 in/36–40 cm from crown of head to heel. Growth lengthwise slows.

★ Your BT may begin to turn this month to be head down (ready for birth).

★ The following are now formed:
   » Senses: your BT will now react to sound and light.
   » Rhythmic breathing patterns.
   » The ability to regulate body temperature.

★ The following continue to form:
   » The respiratory system.
   » The digestive tract.
   » Brain tissue and a larger head to accommodate the brain.
   » Skeleton.
   » Fat.

Your CO

Possible symptoms	Possible causes
Leg cramps	Thought to occur because of the extra weight your CO is carrying or her growing uterus, restricting her blood circulation. Diet may also be a factor.
Mildly swollen ankles, feet, and fingers	Your CO's body is holding more water than usual, and as the day wears on, it gathers in the lowest parts of her body. It is exacerbated by hot weather or if she is spending a lot of time on her feet.
Varicose veins **Hemorrhoids**	The weight of your BT is pressing on the large blood vessels in your CO's pelvis, and hormone changes affecting blood vessels can slow the return of blood to her heart. This causes smaller veins in the pelvis, legs, and rectum to swell.
Shortness of breath	Your CO's uterus is now pushing against her diaphragm.
Increased urination	Your CO's uterus is now pushing against her bladder.

CALL THE DOCTOR

 Get your CO emergency medical assistance if she has sudden or severe headache, visual disturbances, or increased swelling in her face, hands, or feet. This could indicate preeclampsia, potentially a very serious condition.

MONTH 8 (weeks 31–35)

THIRD TRIMESTER

Home stretch: BT gains weight rapidly as they prepare for labor

Your BT

- ★ Size: 15.7–18.1 in/40–46 cm from crown of head to heel.
- ★ The following are now formed:
  - » Your BT's body is now all in proportion.
  - » Hearing.
  - » Finger- and toenails.
  - » Pigment in their eyes: your BT has blue eyes now, but this may later change.
- ★ The following continue to form:
  - » Fat: your BT will gain about half a pound every week until week 38 and will become less wrinkly as they fill out.
  - » Skeleton: their skeleton continues to harden, but their head remains pliable to enable it to pass through your CO's birth canal. Soft spots—or fontanelles—will remain on your BT's head for up to 18 months before their skull fully fuses together.
  - » Immune system.

COMMANDO DAD TOP TIP

Do not worry about touching your BT's fontanelle, or soft spot, after they're deployed. Although the skull is not fully fused, their brain isn't exposed in any way. A thick, protective membrane is what actually puts the "soft" in soft spot.

Your CO

Possible physical changes	Possible causes
A different walking gait, more like a waddle	Your CO's center of balance has shifted to accommodate her growing uterus, and as labor approaches, her pelvic joints will loosen, ready for labor. Together, these will make your CO unstable. This causes muscle strain and can cause your CO to waddle. This may be even more pronounced when your BT drops into your CO's pelvis (see page 34).

Possible symptoms	Possible causes
Lower back pain	Strain on your CO's body and/or poor posture.
Tingling or numbness in the pelvic region	Thought to be caused by the pelvic joints loosening, ready for labor.
Pelvic pain, which may make it difficult to get around	Pelvic girdle pain or symphysis pubis dysfunction is caused by a misalignment or stiffness of your CO's pelvic joints at either the back or front of her pelvis. It is common, but the severity varies widely. Your CO should speak to her midwife or doctor to discuss treatment and techniques to manage the pain and discomfort.
Braxton Hicks contractions: your CO's uterus hardens and contracts	Your CO's body is beginning to practice for labor, but these types of contractions do not open the cervix and therefore they are completely safe. When they last for a long time and/or feel intense, they are sometimes described as "false labor."

COMMANDO DAD TOP TIP
Once your BT reaches 37 weeks, they are considered full term. See "How to Recognize Labor" (page 102) in *Chapter 6: Deployment Day.*

MONTH 9 (weeks 36–40)

THIRD TRIMESTER
Rapid weight gain as your BT prepares for labor

ADVICE FROM
THE FRONT LINE

"I guess the most important thing any Commando Dad can do for his CO is to just be there. Whether it's a shoulder rub or making a cup of tea, just be there. It's not just about earning brownie points—it really makes you feel like you've done something to help."
DAVE BOATWRIGHT

Your BT

★ Size: 18.5–20 in/47–51 cm from crown of head to heel.
★ The following are now formed:
  » All organ systems.
  » Brain.
  » Lungs.
  » The skeleton is hardened (excluding the head).
  » Muscles: arm and leg muscles are strong (as your CO will know from feeling your BT move around).
  » Reflexes are now fully coordinated, so they can blink, turn their head, and grasp firmly.
★ Lanugo, the fine hair that covered your baby, begins to be shed, though some may remain at birth on the baby's shoulders, folds of skin, and the backs of ears.

Your CO

Possible physical changes	Possible causes
Breasts may begin to leak	Your CO is producing colostrum, or "first milk."

Possible symptoms	Possible causes
Less indigestion **Improved breathing** **Increased urination** **Back pain**	Your BT, who is now head down, will "drop" into your CO's pelvis. This is called "lightening." It may give her a heavier feeling in her pelvis, but less pressure just below her ribcage will make it easier to breathe and eat without getting indigestion.
Frustration	Your CO will now be very large, uncomfortable, and eager to go into labor.

ADVICE FROM THE FRONT LINE

"Everyone (and their dog) is only too willing to give you advice during and after the pregnancy—and no two pieces are the same. In the end I had an auto response, 'Thanks, that's very interesting, and I will bear that in mind.' The bottom line is that no two pregnancies are the same and everyone is different—the worst thing I did was try and compare ours to other people's. I probably spent too much time on the Internet reading about what could go wrong instead of concentrating on how amazing it all was."

CALUM BEATT

RECAP AND REFRESH

Chapter 1: New Recruits has provided:

★ A general overview of:
  » The physical changes that your CO may experience.
  » Your BT's development.

★ Information about symptoms that you shouldn't ignore, and when it's necessary to call the doctor. For a more detailed overview about which physical symptoms are normal and which ones aren't, including how to recognize potentially serious problems, both physical (e.g., preeclampsia) and mental (e.g., prenatal depression), see *Chapter 4: Call the Doctor.*

★ There is more information about prenatal scans and appointments in *Chapter 2: Actions on Appointments.*

★ If you and your CO are expecting twins or multiples, you can find additional information about prenatal scans and appointments in the "Multiple Deployments" section of *Chapter 9: Special Ops.*

★ It is essential that you both have the healthiest lifestyle possible. Starting now. Find more information, tips, and advice in *Chapter 3: Fit for Fatherhood.*

ACTIONS ON APPOINTMENTS

Prenatal appointments are a crucial element of pregnancy. They provide you with an essential contact with the medical support team—your midwife, doctors, and sonographers—that is going to help you and your CO through pregnancy and childbirth. Books can provide you with general information about pregnancy; your medical support team can provide specific answers to *your* questions about your CO and BT. Where possible, attend.

By the end of this chapter, you'll have an overview of the prenatal appointments that your CO will be invited to attend throughout pregnancy. It also provides information about childbirth classes: what they are, what's available, and how to access them.

ADVICE FROM
THE FRONT LINE

"Time spent in reconnaissance is seldom wasted."
NICK BURBIDGE

"Try and get to all the appointments if you can. During pregnancy your CO can become . . . let's just say 'not herself,' but if you're there you can make sure you ask the questions you want answers to. Plus it will help you start on the road to bonding with your new baby."
DAN SAXTON

What you need to know:

★ In a single pregnancy with no complications, your CO will receive 8 to 10 appointments and 2 to 3 scans:
  » An initial appointment at 8–12 weeks, followed by appointments at:
    » 16 weeks
    » 25 weeks
    » Every 3 weeks until 34 weeks (weeks 28, 31, and 34)
    » Every other week or so after 34 weeks (weeks 36, 38, 41, or thereabouts)
    » 41 weeks if your BT hasn't deployed
  » Scans typically occur at:
    » 8–14 weeks. This is the "dating scan" where you will see your BT for the first time and be given a reliable date for when they may deploy.
    » 18–22 weeks. This is the "anatomy" scan to confirm that your BT is developing normally.
★ Your CO may require more scans in certain circumstances, such as:
  » Your CO is considered to be at a higher risk of complications.
  » Your CO is expecting twins or multiples. Please see *Chapter 9: Special Ops* for more information about appointments for these multiple deployments.

★ Talk with your manager or HR department to see if they are willing, or able, to let you attend appointments. Read on to see what each scan and appointment involves so that if you can only attend some, you can make an informed choice about which ones would work best for you both.

★ Appointments will give you and your CO not only information about maintaining a healthy pregnancy, but also an opportunity to ask questions.

COMMANDO DAD TOP TIP

You may not be able to attend all appointments, but let your CO know she's still got your support. Call or send a supportive text on the day to let her know you're thinking of her.

ADVICE FROM
THE FRONT LINE

"From the start the biggest benefit I found was to involve myself in everything I could. If you don't, you very quickly start to feel left out when things are mentioned and you don't have a clue what they are talking about. I managed to get to every midwife/doctor appointment and scan. My boss and company were very flexible about this."

PAUL DRAKE

PRENATAL APPOINTMENTS AND SCANS

Although there is a set of scheduled appointments and scans, you or your CO can contact your doctor or midwife at any time if you have any worries or concerns.

Informing your doctor or a midwife

When your CO finds out she is pregnant, she will need to let her doctor or a midwife know, so that she can immediately gain access to the care she needs and can have the first official prenatal appointment scheduled.

This initial contact will enable her to receive information about how to take care of herself and her BT through diet and lifestyle choices. Your CO will need to tell the doctor if any of the following apply:

★ She has preexisting medical conditions, including diabetes and high blood pressure.

★ Anyone in either of your families has previously had a BT with a congenital defect, such as spina bifida.

★ There is a history in either of your families of an inherited disease—for example, sickle cell or cystic fibrosis.

COMMANDO DAD TOP TIP

Your CO will need to go to this visit with a full bladder, as the doctor will want to confirm her pregnancy with their own test, which is more often than not a urine test. However, some clinics or practices may prefer to give a blood test.

ADVICE FROM THE FRONT LINE

"We told close family quite early, but only after the CO had a test at the doctor's. I don't know why, but for some reason having a doctor tell us made it more real, even though, as we are both engineers, we understand that the science in the home tests is essentially the same as what the doctors do."

PHILIP SOWERBY

FIRST APPOINTMENT
Eight to 12 weeks

This is a very busy appointment that involves filling in a lot of paperwork. This appointment could be with your PCP or a midwife. The midwife could be attached to your local hospital or your doctor's practice, or she could be a community midwife. Depending on what's available in your local area, this initial appointment could be held at the hospital, your local midwife-led unit, or your doctor's practice.

This is the doctor's opportunity to get to know your CO and family history (for both of you). She will use this information to determine the level of care for your CO and whether she needs additional support from a specialist.

Your CO will be asked about:

* **The date of her last period.** This is an indicator of your CO's due date. See "Dating scan" (page 44) for more information about the scan that will be able to more accurately predict the date your BT will deploy.
* **Previous miscarriages and abortions.**
* **Family history.** This may—or may not—have a bearing on your pregnancy. Your CO will be advised of screening tests for conditions and given information to allow you both to make a balanced judgment about whether to take them or not.
* **Age.** Very young mothers and mothers over 35 may need additional support.
* **Where she works.** Your midwife will want to determine whether your CO's job may pose a risk to her pregnancy.
* **Her lifestyle.** The main concern will be if you or your CO smoke and if your CO drinks alcohol. Both of these can affect your BT's health and development. You and your CO are in this together. If you're not already, you both need to adopt a healthy lifestyle: eating well, no drinking, and no smoking. Getting fit or maintaining fitness levels is also good for both of you. See *Chapter 3: Fit for Fatherhood* for tips and advice.

Your midwife will want to take some important measurements and give your CO some important tests:

* Your CO will have her **height and weight** measured and her body mass index (BMI) calculated.
  * » A high BMI (over 30) may indicate that your CO has a higher risk of developing gestational diabetes and other complications. Your CO may need additional medical support.

» A low BMI (under 18) may indicate that your CO is at risk of giving birth to a BT with a low birth weight. Your CO may need additional medical support.

★ **Blood samples** will be taken to be tested for:
  » Immunity to rubella (German measles)
  » Iron levels (to see if your CO is anemic)
  » Her blood group, and whether she is rhesus positive or negative
  » Additional screening for HIV, STDs (chlamydia, gonorrhea, and syphilis), and hepatitis B and C

★ An optional screening for Down syndrome and spina bifida, if they are offered in your local area and if your CO wants to have them. Screening for Down syndrome may also involve a nuchal translucency scan (more information follows).

★ **A urine sample** will be taken at this and all subsequent appointments, to check for the following:
  » Protein, which can be an indicator of a number of issues including a urine infection, high blood pressure, a kidney disorder, or diabetes. From 20 weeks and beyond, protein may also indicate preeclampsia, a potentially serious condition characterized by protein in the urine and the onset of high blood pressure.
  » Blood, which could indicate an infection.
  » Glucose, which could indicate gestational diabetes (meaning your CO's blood sugar level is too high).

★ At this and all subsequent appointments, your CO's blood pressure will be taken. High blood pressure can be an indicator of preeclampsia.

Your doctor or midwife will also want to understand your CO's plans for her pregnancy and childbirth. This includes:

★ **Where your CO would like to have your BT.** Your doctor or midwife will be able to provide information about all the different options available in your area.

★ **If you would like to attend childbirth classes.** Your doctor or midwife will be able to provide details of available classes in your area. (More information about childbirth classes follows.)

★ **If your CO intends to breastfeed.** It's good to get as much information about breastfeeding as possible, so that you and your CO can make a judgment about whether it will work for your unit. Your midwife will be able to provide you with information about breastfeeding and also whether there are local classes or support groups in your area.

Your doctor or midwife will also be able to provide your CO with key information that she needs to know for the journey ahead. This includes:

★ **Your BT's development.**

★ **How your CO can ensure optimal health during pregnancy.** This includes lifestyle, diet, vitamins, and exercise.

★ **Prenatal care.** Forthcoming appointments and scans, screening tests, prenatal education, and breastfeeding classes.

At the end of the appointment, your CO will receive notes that record the results of the tests (with the exception of the blood test, which will need to be sent to a lab for testing) and a plan of care.

EMOTION ALERT

Scans and tests can be stressful. These feelings may be exacerbated if you and your CO have a history of miscarriage or if you are already feeling anxious about the pregnancy. When waiting for medical staff or test results, try to remain calm. Don't anticipate outcomes.

If you do get a result that you may not have expected, don't panic. Ask any questions you need to to fully understand the implications. If you and your CO have to make a difficult decision based on a test result, try to remain calm. Remember to listen to each other.

SCAN: Dating scan
Eight to 14 weeks

This first ultrasound scan will provide a more reliable due date for your BT's deployment. It will also confirm whether your CO is expecting a single BT or twins or multiples. It provides an opportunity to screen for possible abnormalities.

This is also an opportunity for both of you to see your BT for the first time. At 8 weeks you will be able to discern your BT's head and limb buds, and a heartbeat. At this moment, everything becomes very, very real.

EMOTION ALERT

Nothing can prepare you for how you will feel when you see your BT for the first time. It was a life-changing moment for me that triggered really powerful emotions that I wasn't expecting. Be prepared.

ADVICE FROM
THE FRONT LINE

"I was not prepared for the first scan. I had seen other people's photos before and paid little attention, to be honest—including my own sister's BT. But seeing your own little one moving in real time is an unforgettable moment."
PHIL SOWERBY

TELLING PEOPLE

You may feel after 12 weeks, when the first trimester is over and the risk of miscarriage is reduced, that you want to start to tell people. Your nearest and dearest may already have noticed that your CO is behaving differently and that your lifestyle may have changed—both giving up smoking or drinking, for example—and so may suspect. Don't be disappointed if this is the case. They're happy for you both. Enjoy it.

EMOTION ALERT

It can be quite difficult to tell your own parents that you're going to become a parent yourself. It may bring up all kinds of emotions, depending on the relationship that you have with them. Bear in mind that this is a life-changing moment for them too, as they are going to become grandparents to your BT. If this is the first time that they have become grand-parents, it may take a while to sink in.

ADVICE FROM THE FRONT LINE

"I am very matter-of-fact about these sorts of things, but I was still feeling nervous and proud to be telling my dad. Not for any macho reason of 'look Dad, I've got swimmers!' but because it's a real-life experience that we can share and brings us closer together."
PHIL SOWERBY

SCAN: Nuchal translucency scan or triple test (if required)
Eleven to 14 weeks

Both the nuchal translucency scan and triple test are designed to indicate the probability of there being a problem. It will not determine whether your BT will definitely be affected, but will help you both decide whether you wish to have a diagnostic (invasive) test to be certain. See "Diagnostic tests" (page 46) for more information.

Nuchal translucency scan

Sometimes known as the nuchal fold scan, the nuchal translu-cency scan, like all scans, is optional. It is a screening test that measures the amount of fluid under the skin at the back of your BT's neck as an indicator of chromosomal abnormalities such as Down syndrome. Your CO will have this scan only if it is offered in your area and if she opts to have it. If she does choose to have it, then it is possible for it to be carried out at the same time as the dating scan (as long as the scan is between 11 and 14 weeks). It is advisable that she attend this scan with you or a friend or relative for support.

Triple test

This is an alternative to a nuchal translucency scan that some hospitals offer instead. It is a blood test that measures levels of three substances in your CO's blood:

- ★ **Alpha-fetoprotein (AFP):** a protein produced by your BT's liver
- ★ **Unconjugated estriol (UE):** a protein produced in your CO's placenta and in your BT's liver
- ★ **Human chorionic gonadotropin (hCG):** a hormone produced by your CO's placenta

The blood needs to be sent away for analysis, and results are usually back in 7 to 10 days. It may be advisable for your CO to pick up the results with you or a friend or relative for support.

Diagnostic tests

Diagnostic tests help determine the chances of your BT's being born with a chromosomal disorder. Your CO may be offered these if the nuchal translucency scan indicated the possibility of abnormalities, if either of you has a close family member with a chromosomal condition, or if your CO is over 35. Diagnostic tests do carry a slight risk of miscarriage, and you will both need to discuss and understand the pros and cons with your doctor or midwife before proceeding.

Diagnostic tests are invasive; they involve inserting a needle into your CO's uterus (after local anesthetic has been administered) to extract cells that can be examined and tested for a number of conditions:

- ★ CV or chorionic villus sampling: cells from the placenta—chorionic villi—are removed for testing. This test can be taken between 10 and 13 weeks.

★ Amniocentesis: cells that your BT has shed are in the amniotic fluid; a sample of this fluid is removed for testing. This test can be taken between 15 and 20 weeks.

SECOND APPOINTMENT
Sixteen weeks

★ Your CO will be able to review, discuss, and record the results of the blood tests taken at the initial appointment and also any screening tests.

★ Your CO will have her blood pressure measured and her urine tested for protein, blood, and glucose.

★ Your doctor or midwife will also be able to answer any questions you both may have about the next scan—the anatomy scan.

★ Your doctor or midwife may be able to pick up your BT's heartbeat from around 16 weeks, using a handheld Doppler (a fetal monitor) that amplifies the sound so that you and your CO will also be able to hear it. Less often, the doctor may have a Pinard stethoscope (an ear trumpet). Be aware that your BT's heartbeat will be racing: their heart typically beats between 120 and 160 beats per minute, compared to our 60 to 100.

 COMMANDO DAD TOP TIP
There is a huge difference between not being able to hear a fetal heartbeat and a fetal heartbeat not being present. Although it is obviously very reassuring for you and your CO to be able to hear your BT's heartbeat, sometimes, depending on a number of factors, it may not be possible. These factors include the size of your BT, their position, the position of the placenta, and the position of your CO's uterus.

SCAN: Anatomy scan
Eighteen to 22 weeks

This scan will confirm whether your BT is developing normally. This is also the scan where you can find out the sex of your BT, should you choose to. Let the sonographer know either way beforehand.

This scan is also another milestone at which to tell people who may not already know about your BT, and also to begin to buy the things you'll need. For tips on what to buy, see *Chapter 5: Report to the Stores.*

EMOTION ALERT
This is a milestone, and you may feel relief and confidence that everything is progressing as it should. It could also be the point where you hear that there may be an issue. In this instance, ask any questions you need to to fully understand the implications. If you and your CO need to progress to further tests, try to remain calm. Do not anticipate outcomes. Accept the help and support that is offered.

THIRD APPOINTMENT
Twenty-five weeks
- ★ Your CO will have her blood pressure measured and her urine tested for protein, blood, and glucose.
- ★ Your CO will be given a glucose test to determine if she has gestational diabetes. She will be given a sugary solution to drink, and one hour later her blood sugar will be checked.
- ★ The doctor or midwife will:
  - » Measure your CO's uterus to check that everything is developing normally
  - » Give her an abdominal examination—a palpation—by moving her hands over your CO's abdomen
  - » Possibly listen to your BT's heartbeat

FOURTH TO SIXTH APPOINTMENTS
Every 3 weeks between 28 and 34 weeks
- ★ Your CO will have her blood pressure measured and her urine tested for protein, and perhaps blood and glucose.
- ★ The doctor or midwife will:
  - » Measure your CO's uterus to check that everything is developing normally

- » Give her an abdominal examination
- » Possibly listen to your BT's heartbeat
★ If your CO's blood is rhesus negative, she will be offered anti-D treatments. This is an injection that will prevent her body producing antibodies against the rhesus-positive fetus. The first treatment will be offered at 28 weeks and then again at 34 weeks.

SEVENTH APPOINTMENT
Thirty-six weeks

★ Your CO will have her blood pressure measured and her urine tested for protein, and perhaps blood and glucose.
★ Your CO will be tested for Group B strep and retested for HIV. If her Group B strep test is positive, she will need to be administered antibiotics during labor.
★ The doctor or midwife will:
- » Measure your CO's uterus to check that everything is developing normally
- » Give her an abdominal examination and check the position of your BT
- » Possibly listen to your BT's heartbeat
★ Your midwife will also want to give your CO information about:
- » Feeding and caring for your new BT
- » Vitamin K—an optional injection given to your BT after birth to prevent spontaneous bleeding—and screening tests for your newborn baby
- » Your CO's health after your BT is deployed
- » Baby blues—what it is and how your CO can deal with it
- » Postpartum depression—how to recognize and deal with it

COMMANDO DAD TOP TIP
There is no such thing as a stupid question. This is your first BT, whereas the professionals have taken an active part in many, many births. If you think of a question when you're not in an appointment, jot it down or make a note on your phone and keep it close.

ADVICE FROM
THE FRONT LINE

"Go to every appointment you can. Simple. Your CO is going through a lot of emotions and changes. I had a page full of questions when I went to the appointments. Your CO will be more concerned with the immediate issues, as she should be, and may not remember everything she wanted to ask. Read all the literature you can; you may relate to some of it, may believe or trust none of it, but some of it will stick. The literature is not there to scare you."
JAMES FENWICK

EIGHTH AND NINTH APPOINTMENTS
Thirty-eight and 40 weeks
★ Your CO will have her blood pressure measured and her urine tested for protein, and perhaps blood and glucose.
★ The doctor or midwife will:
  » Measure your CO's uterus to check that everything is developing normally
  » Give her an abdominal examination and check the position of your BT
  » Possibly listen to your BT's heartbeat
★ At the 40 weeks appointment, your CO will be given more information about what happens if her pregnancy lasts longer than 41 weeks.

TENTH APPOINTMENT
Forty-one weeks
★ Your CO will have her blood pressure measured and her urine tested for protein, and perhaps blood and glucose.
★ The doctor or midwife will:
  » Measure your CO's uterus to check that everything is developing normally

» Give her an abdominal examination and check the position of your BT

» Possibly listen to your BT's heartbeat

★ As your BT still hasn't deployed, your CO may be offered an induction, to start her labor artificially. See "Induction" in *Chapter 6: Deployment Day* for more information about different methods of induction.

3D AND 4D SCANS

In addition to the scans already described, you may wish to have a 3D or 4D scan (the fourth dimension being time, meaning you can see your BT moving in real time on the screen). This will need to be arranged separately from the routine prenatal scans.

If you do choose to have this type of scan, the best time is between 26 and 30 weeks. This is because your BT will have a layer of fat (so they'll look like you'd expect a newborn to) but their head won't have gone deep into your CO's pelvis. Be aware that you may not be able to get a view or a picture of your BT's face—this will depend on their position.

THE BIRTH PLAN

You and your CO may want to write a birth plan. This will outline how you both would ideally like the labor and birth to go, including pain relief and where and how your CO would like to give birth. You will also be able to discuss what your role should be during labor. You may decide together with your CO that you won't attend the birth. If only one person is allowed in the delivery room with your CO, she may choose to have a relative or friend with her, for part or all of the labor. Whatever works for your own family unit is the right way. Don't let anyone else judge the decisions you make.

It's important to be aware that your birth plan is just that—a plan—and that like all plans, it may need to change to keep pace with fast-moving events. On the big day, certain facilities may not be available, or there may be complications, or your CO may simply change her mind. If the latter is the case, ensure that your CO does not waste any energy on disappointment or, worse, guilt. Labor is a marathon, not a sprint. Anything your CO needs along the way should be given to her. And quickly.

CHILDBIRTH CLASSES

Childbirth classes are designed to provide your CO and you with more information about pregnancy, labor, looking after a newborn BT, and what help and support is available to you. They also give you and your CO an opportunity to meet other local parents-to-be in an informal setting.

Although called a class, they're not there to teach you and your CO the perfect way to deliver and look after your BT. There isn't a perfect way. Rather, it's an interactive experience where you get the benefit of an expert sharing information with you, and you get to ask lots of questions. Remain open-minded and gather as much information about the options available to you as possible, so that you can make informed choices.

Childbirth classes are not mandatory, and it is up to you and your CO to find out what's available and to register yourselves in a course that best suits you. It is advisable to register well in advance to make sure you get a spot. You or your CO should ask about childbirth classes available in your local area in one of your earliest appointments and also check out websites that include local listings for childbirth classes.

You can attend as many different classes as you want to, but be aware that most have associated fees. You might want to supplement your childbirth classes with specialist workshops dedicated to topics such as breastfeeding, multiple births, water birth, or home birth, for example.

"I was pretty clueless about the whole thing and learned A LOT going to the childbirth classes. It was a great place to meet other prospective dads who were in the same frame of mind as me—that is, freaking out a little bit."

NEIL WHITE

Timing

If your CO is having a single BT, she ideally needs to have childbirth classes from her third trimester (from 27 weeks onward) and have them completed by week 39. If your CO is carrying more than one BT, she is likely to deliver early and so will need to complete childbirth classes sooner: 34 weeks for twins and 30 weeks for multiple births. For more information on prenatal care for COs carrying more than one BT, see the "Multiple Deployments" section in *Chapter 9: Special Ops.*

"It's a good idea to attend childbirth classes from a social and support side of things. I don't come from, or work in, the place that we now live in and had our son. So the social group for me and Katherine was pretty small. Having a group of people all thinking the same things, asking the same questions, and able to express concern and support for each other through pregnancy and the first year (so far) has been invaluable. We still meet up for play dates, and we've had a couple of dads' nights out too, which has helped us stay in touch with the rest of the world!"

NICK DAWSON

Online

Online classes are increasingly available and getting more sophisticated. It's possible to watch high-quality video (and rewatch it later) and possibly chat online to other parents-to-be and midwives. They're not local, so you and your CO will need to speak to your midwife or doctor about local maternity facilities, but they will cover the main topics. Securing a place on them shouldn't be a problem, and it removes the issue of whether you can attend all of the classes. Some providers do charge a fee.

Finding the right childbirth class

What childbirth class you and your CO sign up for will depend on what you want to get out of them. Here are some things to bear in mind:

★ Most classes will cover the main topics, although some may focus on certain aspects more than others:
  » Health and well-being of your CO and BT
  » Labor and childbirth
  » Advice on breathing and relaxation techniques
  » Pain relief options
  » Early parenthood: physical changes and caring for a newborn BT, including breastfeeding
★ You may wish to find a childbirth class that supports your circumstances; for example:
  » Twins or multiples
  » Very young mothers
★ You may wish to find a childbirth class that supports the decisions you and your CO have made about labor and childbirth. Or you may wish to sign up for specialist classes or workshops to supplement your childbirth classes. For example:
  » Active birth: where your CO stays active during labor to achieve a natural birth
  » Home birth
  » Water birth
  » Natural (that is, drug-free) birth
  » Cesarean birth

» HypnoBirthing: where your CO uses self-hypnosis during labor and childbirth

★ Exercise all the usual caution if signing up for an independent course, and check the experience and qualifications of the course provider.

ADVICE FROM
THE FRONT LINE

"The childbirth classes provided more than information—they provided friendships. People like you, going though the same fears, apprehensions, and questions."
MARK BAKER

"Having a BT on the way is an amazing experience, and you should embrace it."
JAMES FENWICK

RECAP AND REFRESH

Chapter 2: Actions on Appointments has provided:

★ A review of scans and appointments your CO will need to attend. The list of tests, scans, and check-ups presented in the chapter may seem daunting, but they will soon become routine for you and your CO.

★ Information about childbirth classes and how to sign up for them. Register early.

★ You may wish to start buying things for your BT after the first trimester has ended or your CO has had the anatomy scan. For advice on what to buy, see *Chapter 5: Report to the Stores*.

★ If you and your CO are expecting twins or multiples, you can find additional information about prenatal scans and appointments in the "Multiple Deployments" section of *Chapter 9: Special Ops*.

CHAPTER 3

FIT FOR FATHERHOOD

THE BRIEF

Few occasions in life will present you with a greater opportunity to take stock of your life than finding out you're going to be a dad. Grab it with both hands. Take a long hard look at your levels of health and fitness and your lifestyle. This is to enable you to be fit not only for the impending rigors of early fatherhood, but also for the many years of fathering adventures that lie ahead.

THE OBJECTIVE

By the end of this chapter you will know about changes you can easily make to your lifestyle, fitness levels, and eating habits that will help you to be fit for fatherhood. If you're already a perfect physical specimen, your challenge will be to maintain that; the early stages of fatherhood are a prime time to put on weight due to poor diet and physical inactivity. See page 63 for tips on fitting in exercise around family commitments.

"Something I tell other would-be fathers is that they need to look after themselves. Nutrition and exercise are important, as well as getting as much sleep as possible. I kept exercising before and after."
NEIL WHITE

LIFESTYLE

SMOKING

If you smoke, stop. There's never going to be a better incentive. Cigarette smoke, either from your CO smoking directly or from her breathing in your secondhand smoke, restricts the essential oxygen supply to your developing BT. This can cause a whole host of problems, which you can prevent. I can't tell you that giving up cigarettes will be easy, but I can assure you that it will be easier to live with than causing harm to your unborn BT. If your CO smokes, she needs to stop too.

How can I practically help my CO to give up smoking?

★ Support and encourage her. The more stressed she is, the more likely she is to feel she needs a cigarette.
★ If you're smoking, stop.
★ Remove physical traces of smoking from your home and car: cigarettes, ashtrays, lighters, and so on.
★ Avoid social situations where people may be smoking; replace them with ones where smoking is less likely.
★ Tell family and friends and ask them to be supportive.

DRINKING

Now is a good time to review your drinking habits. Even if you are a light or moderate drinker, you'll be pleasantly surprised by the effect that cutting back or removing alcohol will have on your sleep (it will improve immediately), your energy levels, and perhaps even your weight. But cutting down on drinking has long-term benefits, too—reducing your risk of health issues such as high blood pressure, heart disease, cancer, and liver cirrhosis.

As backup support to your CO, you're also going to want to support her as she cuts out alcohol altogether or reduces consumption to the lowest levels.

ADVICE FROM THE FRONT LINE

"I cut right down on my drinking before and certainly after my BT was born. I wanted to be clear-headed and to be able to support my wife in the lead-up to the birth—especially nearer the due date. And once the wee fellow was born, I didn't drink for the first few weeks, as sleep was at a premium and we didn't know when we would be woken up. The last thing I wanted was to be fuzzy-headed in the middle of the night when my mind had to be on the little BT."

CALUM BEATT

If your CO drinks alcohol when pregnant, it crosses the placenta into the bloodstream of your unborn BT. The American College of Obstetrics and Gynecology (ACOG) encourages women to avoid alcohol entirely throughout their pregnancy. Based on current findings, no amount of alcohol consumption is considered safe during pregnancy. The only way to guarantee there are no ill effects is for your CO not to drink at all.

Excessive drinking can have devastating effects on your unborn BT. Fetal alcohol syndrome (FAS) can cause facial deformities and problems with physical and emotional development.

If your CO thinks she may benefit from support to help her stop drinking, she can speak to her doctor or midwife.

What is one unit?

A unit is a measure of alcohol, but most drinks are usually over one unit. Some examples:

★ Small (0.8 oz/25 ml) measure of liquor (vodka, gin, rum, whiskey, etc.): 1 unit
★ Small (4.3 oz/125 ml) glass of wine: 1.5 units
★ A bottle of beer: 1.7 units

How can I practically help my CO to stop—or reduce—drinking?
★ Support and encourage her.
★ Cut down the amount that you drink, or stop altogether.
★ Avoid social situations where people may be drinking and replace them with ones where drinking is less likely.
★ Tell family and friends and ask them to be supportive.

FITNESS

Fatherhood requires strength and stamina, and there's no better time than right now to adopt a healthier lifestyle and improve your fitness. This will not only deliver the obvious health benefits, but also help you better deal with the hectic lifestyle of a new dad.

ADVICE FROM THE FRONT LINE

"I'm not a particularly fit guy, but I took the opportunity to get fit before the arrival of our BT by signing up for the Great North Run. I found that with increased fitness levels I am able to cope better with less sleep, manage stress considerably better, effectively keep base camp in order, and provide support to my wife."
STEVE COOPER

The most important thing you need when getting—and staying—fit is the right mindset. It's what will get you going in the early days and keep you going as you incorporate long-term changes into your lifestyle. Being fit isn't just about achieving a certain goal (although goals can be great motivators); it's about habitually making better choices when it comes to diet, exercise, and lifestyle. Don't be put off by this. Good habits may be hard to form, but they're easy to live with. Keep at it.

ADVICE FROM THE FRONT LINE

"This was a major part of the pregnancy for me—I was determined to be in the best shape of my life for when baby arrived. However, I ensured that my routine was tailored to the wife so that it didn't interfere with me being able to look after and support her."
PAUL HOPE

Maintaining fitness

When your trooper deploys, you will need to master the art of fitting in exercise around your family commitments. Time is going to be in short supply, especially in the first few months when your BT is getting into a schedule.

"I've always played football/boxed/Ju Jitsu. I fully believe in healthy body, healthy mind. I believe it will help me cope with my child's demands and keep me fit and healthy as they grow up. I want to be active with them and maybe coach the football team in later years (of course, they may not like football!)."
GRANT MILLS

★ **Go out and about with your BT.** In the early days, this could be just getting out for a walk in the fresh air with your BT and CO. Sorties can become more adventurous as time passes: you can go hiking, jogging, and cycling with your BT. Try to increase the intensity during your shorter missions. There is lots of evidence that vigorous intensity exercise is much better for maintaining and increasing fitness than slow plodding exercise. You should just be able to hold a conversation during your fast walks.

"I've been going swimming with my BT as soon as she had had her first jabs; the confidence she now has even at 13 weeks is amazing. It also gives me real one-on-one quality time with her, which is the best thing ever. It also makes bath time far more fun!"
ANDY LONG

"My plan is to get a cycle trailer to take my BT out on the bike as soon as she is old enough."
KEVIN S

★ **If you're at work, try to fit exercise into your schedule:**
  » Getting to work:
    » Cycle to work if possible.
    » If commuting, get off the bus or train one stop earlier and walk the difference. Park the car farther away from the office and walk in.
  » At work, keep physically active. Take the stairs, walk to your colleagues' desks rather than phoning them, and stand as much as possible. Standing doubles the amount of energy that your body uses.
  » If you can get an hour at lunch, see if there is a local gym that you can use, or get out and go for a walk or a jog.

★ **If you're at home:**
  » Become more efficient at exercising. Create—or find—a 15-minute routine that allows you to give yourself a total body workout. Fifteen minutes is the optimum amount of time because even a very young BT will nap for 15 minutes.
  » Do exercise that requires little—or no—equipment: sit-ups, press-ups, skipping, and squats are all fabulous exercises that you can perform in confined spaces at a moment's notice. And that may be all you have. Adopt an exercise lifestyle routine in the same way you will be adopting new routines with your BT.
  » Get exercise equipment you can use at home and be disciplined enough to use it.

★ **If you are training for an event.** Ideally, you're going to need the full support of your CO, not only for her help in looking after your BT while you train, but also as a motivating force to help you to stick to your schedule. This can be tricky if you need to train at times that you previously spent with your partner (especially if you are training for an event and your training time is increasing). If this is an issue for you, tackle it now. It is not going to go away. Here's how I did it:
  » I explained to my CO why I really wanted to train and compete.

» I worked to ensure that she had as much "free" time as I had training time. This is especially important as your CO is going to need time away from your BT. Taking care of a new-born BT is a physically and emotionally demanding job.

» I stuck it out and proved I was serious.

If you do need to train away from base camp, avoid busy times in the family day—mealtimes, bedtime, etc.—as all hands need to be on deck then. If you are working, be aware that your CO may be looking forward to your getting home so that she can have a break from looking after your BT and also spend time with you. Either get up early and create time at the start of the day (I prefer this) or be prepared to go out in the evening when your BT is asleep. Although sometimes you may find it hard to get out to train, you will feel so much better afterward.

Maintaining or improving your fitness is essential for your own well-being as well as for that of those around you. Maintaining a range of endurance and strength will help you in the future with your BT, whether lifting them around the house or playing in the park.

NUTRITION

A good diet is a long-term investment in your future. It will keep you healthy and well now, delivering many benefits such as more energy, better sleep, and increased concentration. And it will also reduce your risk of developing illness (e.g., cancer, heart disease) later on. For your CO, a good diet is obviously essential, as she needs to keep herself healthy not only to cope with the rigors of pregnancy and motherhood, but also to help your BT develop and grow.

Eating for two

Your CO may feel hungrier than normal because of the demands on her body, but "eating for two" is a myth. On average, a CO will need to eat only about 300 calories more each day (although your midwife can advise your CO based on her personal circumstances). Quantity isn't really the issue so much as quality. The good news is that you can both share the same healthy diet, and ensure that you, your CO, and your BT all have the nourishment you need.

 COMMANDO DAD TOP TIP

In the early weeks, your CO's eating habits may go awry as her body gets used to soaring hormones and a heightened sense of taste and smell causes food aversions and cravings. You may be concerned if she is craving unhealthy foods, full of saturated fat and sugar. You're right to be concerned, as your CO and BT need a balanced diet in order to thrive, but tread carefully. Your CO is going through a huge period of change, and she does not need to be lectured on a healthy diet. What she does need is support from you to indulge her unhealthy cravings a little, and her healthy cravings a lot.

Try to find alternatives where possible. For example, my wife craved spinach and tomatoes, but she wanted them on a pizza, two or three times a day. Through trial and error we found that wilted spinach and garlic, and a glass of tomato juice with Worcestershire sauce, curbed the cravings for pizza. It also helped that I followed a healthy diet too. She knew she had my support 100% and that if our diet was good for us, it was going to be good for our BT.

If your CO is making only unhealthy food choices, especially beyond those first few weeks, then encourage her to speak to her midwife or doctor for advice. If she has cravings for nonfood items (a condition called "pica") then she should not indulge these without first seeking medical advice, as they are potentially harmful to her and your BT.

ADVICE FROM THE FRONT LINE

"I wish I had known the dietary needs for mother and child—my partner developed gestational diabetes, which could have been avoided through diet."
RON MURRAY

Food groups

Nutritionists advise the following recommended daily intake of certain types of foods:

Portion plate containing all the food groups you, your CO, and your BT need.

Food group	Purpose	Types of food	Amount
Grains Cereals	Energy Fiber Vitamins Minerals	• All breads: white, whole wheat, multigrain, quick • Rice • Grains: e.g., wheat, corn, barley, buckwheat, millet, oats • Pasta, noodles, couscous	• These should form the main part of your meal. • Include at least one food from this group at every meal. • Whole grains are best.
Fruits and vegetables	Fiber Vitamins Minerals Source of antioxidants	• All fruit and vegetables: fresh and frozen • Fruit and vegetable juices • Peas, beans, and sweet corn	• Eat at least 5 portions of fruit and vegetables a day, prioritizing vegetables over fruit, as they have the same health benefits but less sugar.
Milk and dairy	Calcium Protein Vitamins Minerals	• Milk • Cheese • Yogurt • Farmer cheese	• Eat 3 portions a day. • Choose low-fat dairy products. They have the same amount of calcium.
Meat, fish, and nondairy protein	Protein Vitamins Minerals Fiber (legumes)	• Meat: beef, pork, lamb • Fish: fresh, frozen, and canned • Eggs • Poultry: chicken and turkey • Legumes: beans, peas, lentils • Nuts • Soy protein	• Include foods from this category every day. • Aim to include at least 2 portions of fish per week, especially oily. • Choose lean cuts of meat; remove any visible fat from the meat or the skin from poultry.
Fats	Energy Vitamins	• Butter, margarine, low-fat spread, cooking oils, lard, etc. • Mayonnaise, oily dressings • Cream	• Limit this group.

Processed foods

If something has been done to your food before you buy it at the market, it has been processed. Try to avoid processed food if possible. If you eat food in its natural state, your body can recognize it and use it efficiently. The more processed your food is, the more likely it is to contain high levels of sugar, salt, and saturated fat. They are typically high in calories.

There are obvious processed foods that we all know to avoid: cookies, cakes, sodas, chocolate, sweets, chips, and pastries. However, there are foods that we may not necessarily think of as "processed" that we should also limit. These include:

★ White pasta, rice, and breads; eat whole grain versions.
★ Fruit and vegetable juices: the fiber has been removed.
★ Breakfast cereals: check labels for sugar and sodium content.

Foods your CO should avoid

There are certain foods that your CO should avoid during pregnancy, as they are thought to increase the chance of getting listeriosis (when the food is contaminated by bacteria called listeria). These include:

★ Soft cheeses (Brie, Camembert, blue cheese, soft goat cheese, etc.)
★ Unpasteurized milk
★ Raw or undercooked eggs (homemade mayonnaise contains raw egg, for example); all eggs must be cooked all the way through, with no runny yolks and a solid white
★ Raw or undercooked meat (every piece of meat must be cooked thoroughly—no "pink" meat)
★ Pâté (even vegetarian varieties)

Your CO is at an increased risk of developing listeriosis because her body's defenses are weaker and therefore less able to resist the listeria bacteria. Use caution. Some countries also advise that pregnant women avoid the following foods:

★ Cooked, sliced deli meats
★ Raw, smoked fish, including smoked salmon

DOCTOR: STAND BY
Call your medical support team if your CO has eaten any of the foods just listed, or inadequately reheated chilled food, and shows early symptoms of listeria infection. These are flu-like symptoms: fever, headache, tiredness, aches, and pains.

Other high-risk foods
Some foods can contain harmful bacteria and viruses that can cause food poisoning. This will not harm your BT, but will make life miserable for your CO, as symptoms include vomiting and diarrhea. She will already be avoiding some foods that can cause food poisoning, including raw or undercooked meat, raw eggs, soft cheese, pâté, and unpasteurized milk. Other foods include:
★ Raw shellfish (including mussels, lobster, crab, prawns, scallops, and clams); cold, precooked prawns and shrimp can be eaten
★ Prepacked sandwiches

Too much vitamin A could potentially harm your BT. Your CO needs to avoid fish liver oil supplements or any supplements containing vitamin A (see page 70 for supplements that your CO can take during pregnancy). Foods rich in vitamin A include:
★ Liver
★ Liver products such as liver pâté or liver sausage

Certain types of fish contain high levels of mercury, which may damage your BT's developing nervous system and should be avoided completely. These include:
★ Shark
★ Marlin
★ Swordfish

Other types of fish containing mercury can be eaten, but in limited amounts. These include:

★ Tuna
   » No more than 2 tuna steaks a week
   » Four medium-sized cans of tuna a week
★ Oily fish (salmon, mackerel, sardines, and trout)
   » No more than 2 portions a week

COMMANDO DAD GOLDEN RULES FOR FOOD PREPARATION

★ In addition to limiting or avoiding certain foods, you also need to take care when storing or preparing food. Ensure that your CO's food is cooked until steaming hot throughout. This is especially true if she is eating reheated food or packaged meals.
★ Keep your fridge temperature below 41°F/5°C. She must not eat any perishable food that has been out of the fridge for more than 4 hours.
★ She must not eat any food past its "use by" date (not the same as "sell by" or "display until" dates).
★ All raw fruit and vegetables must be washed thoroughly before use.

Supplements

Even with a diet rich in vitamins and minerals, your CO may need to take pregnancy supplements to ensure that she gets the following nutrients. She can check amounts with her doctor or midwife:

★ Vitamin D every day throughout pregnancy and breastfeeding
★ Folic acid every day, until she is at least 12 weeks pregnant
★ Iron
★ Vitamin C, which among other benefits will help your CO's body absorb iron
★ Calcium

Pregnancy supplements are available from a number of sources; your CO can ask your doctor or midwife for more information. Your CO will need to make sure that she doesn't take a tablet including vitamin A (or retinol), as high levels could harm your BT.

AN ARMY MARCHES ON ITS STOMACH

We all know that home-cooked food is best, but it's hard to get motivated to start cooking from scratch when it's the end of a long day and you're already hungry. While takeout might be a nice treat once in a while, it's not a healthy—or cheap—option, so don't put yourself in that situation. Get organized in advance:

★ **When you do have time to cook, make extra portions and freeze them.** This is good practice now and when your BT deploys. You'll be able to take your evening meal out of the freezer in the morning and pop it into a bowl in the fridge to defrost—basically, your own takeout meal, but one where you know all of the ingredients that went into it.

My favorites for this are curries, chilis, and stews, as the flavor actually seems to improve once they have been defrosted and reheated. When you freeze them, remember to label them clearly, as freezing is the great leveler: it makes everything look the same. When you're reheating these meals, remember to ensure they are steaming hot, and do not refreeze.

★ **Use frozen vegetables.** They will save you time and energy for prepping accompaniments to your meal.

★ **Master the art of the slow cooker.** The fifteen minutes spent prepping vegetables and searing meat in the morning could be rewarded with a rich stew that evening. Make extra portions and freeze.

★ **Use what you have.** I will often search the Internet for inspiration for a meal, based on what I've got in my fridge and freezer. This is great, because it not only introduces variety into your cooking but also saves you money on wasted food.

★ **Learn to make your own "fast food."** The ultimate fast foods are pasta and noodles. You can make a pasta sauce with about 5 minutes' prep, and a stir-fry will take you 3 minutes longer than it takes to chop the vegetables. For optimum nutrition, use whole grain pasta, noodles, and rice.

Search online for your favorite fast foods to see how easy it would be to make them at home from fresh ingredients. You'll be surprised how easy it is—I guarantee it. See the Resources section on www.commandodad.com for some of my favorite recipes, including pasta sauce, burgers, fajitas, and crispy chicken pieces with healthy fries.

> ### ADVICE FROM THE FRONT LINE
>
> *"I have a simple approach to nutrition. My wife is breastfeeding our BT, I am feeding my wife = what I feed my wife is passed to my baby. We have strictly had vegetables every day, in one form or another. I prepare the evening meal in the morning, which means less to do later in the day when we are both tired."*
> STEVE COOPER

RECAP AND REFRESH

You need to get fit and healthy to cope with the rigors of fatherhood. If you know you could make improvements, make them now. *Chapter 3: Fit for Fatherhood* has provided:

★ Tips for giving up smoking and drinking for both you and your CO.
★ Tips for improving your fitness. Your CO will benefit from exercise too and should keep up her normal daily physical activity as long as she feels comfortable. Her doctor or midwife can answer any questions she might have about exercise, including exercise that she needs to avoid.

★ Nutrition, including golden rules for preparing food for your CO and foods she needs to limit or avoid.
★ Basic healthy meal ideas.

CHAPTER 4

CALL THE DOCTOR

THE BRIEF

Your CO's body has a huge period of change ahead of it. You need to know how to distinguish between a "normal" pregnancy ailment and something more serious that may require urgent medical attention. The information in this chapter is intended for information only—if you have, or your CO has any concerns, she should raise these directly with her midwife or doctor.

THE OBJECTIVE

By the end of this chapter you will have an understanding of what's normal—and what isn't—during pregnancy. You'll know how to spot potentially serious problems, both physical (e.g., preeclampsia) and mental (e.g., prenatal depression).

"Don't be afraid, if something doesn't feel right, to pick up the phone and speak to the hospital. Everyone we came in contact with was great."
DAN SAXTON

SYMPTOMS NOT TO IGNORE

Throughout pregnancy, your CO will have a number of symptoms that, while they may be uncomfortable—even painful—and frustrating, distressing, and sometimes even alarming, are nevertheless considered "normal."

However, there are some symptoms that must not be ignored, as they may indicate a medical problem. These are described here. Confusingly, some of these will occur during a normal pregnancy—for example, morning sickness, swollen feet and ankles, and headaches—and be harmless. However, if these symptoms are persistent and severe, or accompanied by other symptoms, they could indicate a problem. All of the conditions I mention are explained further in the sections "Conditions that require urgent medical attention" and "Pregnancy complications."

If you are in doubt, pick up the phone and call your doctor or midwife.

★ **Vaginal bleeding**
  » Light, painless spotting may be a sign of implantation during early pregnancy and shouldn't cause concern.
  » Heavy bleeding with back or abdominal pain needs immediate medical assistance, as this may indicate a miscarriage.
  » Before 8–10 weeks, if it is accompanied by a severe pain in one side of the lower abdomen it may be a symptom of an ectopic pregnancy.
  » Sudden bleeding in late pregnancy could be a symptom of placenta previa, placental abruption, or premature labor.

★ **Leaking fluid**
   » Leaking clear or straw-colored liquid indicates that your CO's waters could have broken. After 37 weeks this is normal and shouldn't cause concern (although you will need to let your doctor or midwife know, as your BT is not as protected from infection once your CO's waters have broken).
   » Before 37 weeks she will need to be monitored for infection and possibly prepared for premature labor.

★ **Abdominal/pelvic pain or pressure:** Lower back pain
   » Before 37 weeks these may be signs of premature labor.

★ **Increased discharge:** Change in volume or type of discharge
   » After 37 weeks this may be a "show," a sign your CO's body is preparing for labor, and is normal. The cervix is getting ready to dilate, so the jelly-like mucus plug that has sealed it comes out. It may be tinged brown or pink.
   » Prior to 37 weeks this could be a sign of premature labor.

★ **Fever or chills**
   This is often an indicator of infection, especially when accompanied by vomiting, and requires treatment.

★ **Vision problems**
   Blurred vision, double vision, dimming, flashing lights, or "floaters" (spots in her field of vision) for more than two hours could indicate preeclampsia.

★ **Severe headaches**
   Persistent headaches that last more than two or three hours may be a symptom of preeclampsia.

★ **Leg cramps**
   Leg cramps are a normal part of pregnancy, but may indicate a blood clot in her leg (or deep vein thrombosis) when:
   » It is a persistent or severe leg cramp or calf pain in one leg that doesn't ease up when she flexes her ankle.
   » The area is red, swollen, and warm to the touch.

★ **Dizziness**
   Early in pregnancy, severe dizziness, accompanied by vaginal bleeding or severe abdominal pain, could indicate ectopic pregnancy.

★ **Persistent itching**

Itching is a normal part of pregnancy as your CO's skin stretches to accommodate her growing body. However, if she gets intense itchiness all over (probably starting in the palms of her hands and the soles of her feet) and she is in the second or third trimester, this may indicate obstetric cholestasis, a liver condition.

★ **Persistent nausea and/or vomiting**

These can indicate hyperemesis gravidarum—a debilitating condition, sometimes requiring hospitalization.

★ **Swelling**

Sudden or severe swelling in hands, feet, or ankles could indicate preeclampsia.

★ **Urine issues**

Discomfort, pain, stinging, burning when she pees, or little or no urine output could indicate an infection. This will require treatment to prevent its causing more serious problems.

★ **Depression**

» While pregnant: unsurprisingly, many women go through mood swings in pregnancy, but if your CO is persistently down, without any positive feelings to balance it out, and she begins to lose interest in work, relationships, and even her pregnancy, this may indicate prenatal depression.

» After she has given birth: shortly after birth, your CO may experience the "baby blues." However, if this lasts for longer than two weeks and your CO is persistently down or begins to lose interest in the relationship with you or your BT, this may indicate postpartum depression.

★ **Contractions (prior to 37 weeks)**

Late in pregnancy, your CO may experience practice contractions called Braxton Hicks. Real contractions differ from these in the following ways:

» They don't go away. Early contractions may feel like persistent back pain and a crampy period pain.

» Real contractions are felt all over, not just at the front.

» Although they may be irregular to start with, they will get stronger, occur at increasingly shorter intervals, last longer, and become more painful.

» The pain will come in a wave, reaching a peak and then tailing off.

CONDITIONS THAT REQUIRE URGENT MEDICAL ATTENTION

If your CO displays any of the symptoms in the following table, call 911 or take her straight to the hospital. Do not delay. Do not second guess. A doctor needs to make a diagnosis—and take action—quickly.

Condition	Symptoms to look out for in your CO	Potential problems
Preeclampsia Sudden onset of high blood pressure which may be associated with protein in urine	Over 20 weeks pregnant and experiencing: • Severe headaches • Blurred vision • Severe swelling of hands, feet, or ankles • A lot of weight gain • Nausea and vomiting • Abdominal pain	In severe cases, a rapid rise in blood pressure can lead to seizure, stroke, and multiple organ failure and can be fatal to your CO and BT.
Placental abruption A condition when the placenta partly or completely separates from the uterus prior to the BT being born	• Vaginal bleeding or spotting • Your CO's waters break and the fluid is bloody • Tenderness or pain in the abdomen • Back pain • Frequent contractions or a single contraction that doesn't stop	Your BT may be born prematurely, have growth problems, or, in severe cases, die.

Continues

Condition	Symptoms to look out for in your CO	Potential problems
Ectopic pregnancy When a fertilized egg implants outside of your CO's uterus, usually in the Fallopian tube	Between 8 and 10 weeks pregnant and experiencing: • Vaginal bleeding • Sudden, sharp, and persistent pain in one side of her abdomen • Dizziness • Shoulder tip pain (the place where her shoulder meets her arm) • Diarrhea and vomiting	There is a serious risk that the Fallopian tube will rupture (burst). In most cases, it can be successfully repaired or removed. In rare cases, a ruptured Fallopian tube can be fatal to your CO.
Premature labor Labor before 37 weeks, i.e., before your BT is fully developed	Less than 37 weeks pregnant and experiencing: • Increased vaginal discharge • Pelvic pressure and cramping • Back pain radiating to the abdomen • Contractions	Generally, the later in the pregnancy your CO is, the better the chance your BT has of surviving.

PREGNANCY COMPLICATIONS

You will need to draw the following complications to your medical support team's attention:

Condition	Symptoms to look out for in your CO	If not treated
Placenta previa A condition in which the placenta partially or wholly blocks the neck of the uterus, interfering with the normal delivery of your BT	• Sudden and painless bleeding • Abdominal pain (rare)	Depends how far your CO is into her pregnancy. She may need to go to the hospital to be monitored. There is a danger of preterm delivery, and your BT may need to be delivered by cesarean section.

Condition	Symptoms to look out for in your CO	If not treated
Postpartum depression Depression that your CO experiences after your BT is born	• Persistent negative emotions: anxiety, fear, guilt, sadness, or hopelessness • Physical manifestations of anxiety: racing heart, sweating, panic attacks • Crying and irritability • Changes in appetite • Taking no pleasure from being with your BT or feeling hostile toward them or you • Exhaustion and lacking in motivation to do anything	Postpartum depression cannot get better without medical intervention.
Prenatal depression Depression that your CO experiences before your BT is born	• As above, but occurring before your BT is born	Prenatal depression needs to be treated. Some COs go on to develop postpartum depression, but it is not a foregone conclusion.
Hyperemesis gravidarum Excessive vomiting	• Severe and persistent nausea or vomiting • Dehydration	Your CO needs fluids and nutrients to nourish her—and your BT. She may need to go to the hospital and receive nourishment through an IV drip.
Gestational diabetes Too much sugar in the blood during pregnancy	Raised blood sugar (your doctor or midwife always checks your CO's urine for protein, but may also check blood and glucose). There may also be additional blood tests if needed.	Can be managed by diet and possibly insulin injections or metformin, a tablet. If left untreated it can lead to a big baby and an increased risk of premature labor.
Obstetric cholestasis A buildup of bile acids in the blood, producing a persistent itch	• Severe, persistent itching • Tiredness • Mild jaundice	Increased concern for your BT's well-being may mean your CO is induced early, before she is full term.

Taking medication

It's not advisable for your CO to take certain medications—even over-the-counter ones such as acetaminophen—during pregnancy, as they may cause problems.

If your CO has a condition that means she has to take medication regularly, she will need to speak to her doctor as soon as she knows she is pregnant. They will be able to confirm whether the medicine is safe to take, or suggest alternatives.

Your CO will also need to make sure that medical professionals—her doctor, dentist, and so on—know that she is pregnant when they are prescribing her any medicines. It is the same for over-the-counter remedies: she will need to speak to the pharmacist to ensure that the medication she is taking is safe to take during pregnancy.

 COMMANDO DAD TOP TIP

Do not assume that herbal alternatives are safe to take during pregnancy. As with all other medications, you or your CO will need to check with your doctor, midwife, or pharmacist.

RECAP AND REFRESH

Chapter 4: Call the Doctor has provided an overview of normal pregnancy ailments and those that may require medical attention. Do not read this chapter to discover all the things that may go wrong—many things may go right. Worry is a negative emotion that achieves nothing, but to be forewarned is to be forearmed. **If you have any concerns, please discuss them directly with your medical backup team—your doctor and midwife—as they are the medical experts who are there to help you.**

To find more information about normal pregnancy symptoms and when your CO may begin to experience them, please see *Chapter 1: New Recruits.*

REPORT TO THE STORES:

Essential Equipment that You Need to Acquire

THE BRIEF

There is a huge number of products that it is possible to buy for your BT. However, in the beginning they will actually require relatively few things. What they do need is close physical contact, food, warmth, a safe and secure environment, and lots of love. You and your CO will be able to assess your BT's ongoing needs and respond accordingly. There is a set of basics that you'll need to have before you bring your BT home: beyond that, everything else is a bonus. It may be prudent to wait until your CO is in her second trimester, when her pregnancy is well established, before you start to buy things.

THE OBJECTIVE

By the end of this chapter you will have an overview of all the basics that you need to buy to ensure you can meet your BT's clothing, changing, feeding, sleeping, and bathing needs. There's also a list of essentials for your first aid kit, and buying tips for baby carriers, travel systems, strollers, and car seats. That is not to say you can't buy more. If you have the funds and want to buy every gadget and gizmo available, then by all means do. But don't feel that you have to.

ADVICE FROM
THE FRONT LINE

"What do you need to buy? Less than you think!"
SAM WINTERSON

"Buy everything!"
GRANT MILLS

CLOTHING

Baby troopers need to be two things: comfortable and accessible (for many diaper-changing sorties). They need stretchy, soft, warm clothes that can withstand the rigors of repeated washing. Do not underestimate the ability of your BT to generate huge amounts of laundry. As a Commando Dad I am sure you already know your way around a washing machine, but if not, familiarize yourself now. Your BT will need:

★ Ten bodysuits and ten sleepers with snaps. These are practical, comfortable, and easily accessible for changing diapers.
★ Ten sets of socks (beware, they will kick them off on a regular basis).
★ Three pairs of infant mittens to prevent your BT from scratching their own face (beware, they will come off on a regular basis).
★ Three cardigans or cotton jackets. Thin layers are better than very thick clothes.
★ Five cotton hats to keep your BT warm (a lot of heat escapes through the head). If the weather is cold, you will need a soft, warm hat for outdoor wear. Hats should be removed when your BT is indoors.
★ Two baby blankets, sometimes called "receiving blankets." These are smaller than crib blankets and are used for keeping your BT warm throughout the day.

COMMANDO DAD TOP TIP

In the early days, the amount of laundry a new BT generates can quickly become overwhelming. Look up laundromats in your local area so that you can fall back on them if you need to. Dropping off a bag of dirty washing and picking it up again clean, dried, and folded is the nearest thing to magic I think I have ever experienced.

DIAPERS AND CHANGING KIT

* If using disposable diapers, buy the smallest bag of newborn diapers you can find. You won't know if the diapers fit until your BT deploys. Even if they do fit, BTs grow very quickly.
* If using cloth diapers, get up to speed on the different types now. Don't buy too many diapers until you know the weight of your BT.
* Baby wipes or cotton wool.
* Diaper rash cream.
* Wipe-clean changing mat.
* Diaper bags, if desired. Useful, but not essential, for "bomb disposal." Any small plastic bag will serve as a good alternative if you are out of diaper bags. Keep them out of reach of your BT.

KITBAG

You will need a dedicated kitbag to carry around essential supplies for sorties away from base camp. It will need to contain changing and feeding supplies. I advocate using a daypack with outside pockets because they are roomy enough to fit in what you need, comfortable to carry, and easy to access and leave your arms free for your Commando Dad duties. You can use your CO's bag if you wish. For more information about kitbags and packing essential supplies, please see *Commando Dad: A Basic Training Manual for the First Three Years of Fatherhood*.

Here is an essential kit list for taking your newborn BT out on a sortie away from base camp:

★ Wipes
★ Diapers
★ Small jar of diaper rash cream (which also acts as a sunblock and a cream for cuts, grazes, and sunburn)
★ Clean pacifier (if used) with cover
★ Changes of clothes: at least two full sets
★ Antibacterial hand gel
★ Diaper bags or plastic bags
★ Portable, wipe-clean changing mat (or a clean towel will suffice)
★ Basic first aid kit
★ Spare keys to your house/car

COMMANDO DAD TOP TIP

All contents of your basic survival kit are nonperishable. This is intentional. Clear it out often, as it will inevitably become a home for perishable items. I put the contents of my basic survival kit in a plastic bag before putting it in my daypack. This not only protects against inclement weather and spillages but also makes the bag easier to clear out.

ADVICE FROM
THE FRONT LINE

"When my daughter was born, I kept a feeding record. Basically, what times the baby fed, for how long, and which breast. Early on it helped us to get used to the routine and work out whether the baby wanted comfort, food or rest, etc. Secondly, every time the nurse asked, I knew the details. That felt good."
STUART COOPER

FEEDING

Breastfeeding

★ A breast pump is essential if your CO plans to express breast milk. You can buy electric or manual hand pumps, depending on her preference.

★ Breast pads (absorbent pads that tuck into the bra to absorb breast milk that leaks).

★ Nipple cream for sore, cracked nipples.

★ Nursing (breastfeeding) bras.

Bottle feeding

★ Two bottles to begin with. You will need more (8 is a good number to ensure that you always have clean bottles), but before you invest more money, you'll need to establish whether your BT likes the bottle or nipple you have chosen.

★ Spare nipples. Nipples that are torn or deteriorated will need to be discarded immediately as they can harbor germs and could also make the milk flow faster than your BT is ready for.

★ Two bottle brushes that are only ever used for washing these bottles.

★ An insulated bottle carrier, if required: for times when you are out and about, without access to a kitchen, and need to give your BT a warm bottle.

Formula feeding

★ The correct formula for your BT's age. If you have a premature baby, they may benefit from formula milks specially designed to ensure they get the extra nutrients they need. Speak to your doctor or midwife or medical support team for advice.

Sterilization equipment

★ A saucepan (used only for this purpose) and water. You'll need to boil all parts of the bottle for 10 minutes in a saucepan, but be aware that this will wear out nipples quickly. You'll need to balance the costs of new nipples against the cost savings of not needing any special equipment.

★ An electric or microwave steam sterilizer. Usually takes a few minutes, and the bottles can be stored in the sterilizer, keeping them sterile for hours (always check the manufacturer's instructions). If you have a microwave, this is probably the most practical option.

★ A cold-water sterilization solution. This allows you to soak bottles and other equipment from as little as 15 minutes to 24 hours. You will need to buy sterilization tablets or fluid regularly. Check the manufacturer's instructions to see if you'll need to rinse items before use.

SLEEPING

★ A bassinet or crib with a new, snug-fitting (i.e., a gap of no more than ¾ in/2 cm) mattress. Gaps around the mattress can be dangerous. You can use a bassinet or crib that has been used before as long as it can be thoroughly cleaned, but do not use a secondhand mattress, as it may pose a health risk.

★ A room thermometer. The ideal temperature for your BT's room is between 65 and 70°F/18 and 21°C. Set your thermostat within this range now so that you can get used to what this temperature actually feels like.

★ Baby monitors, if you wish to use them.

★ Three crib sheets that either are fitted (with elastic corners) or can be tucked in well.

★ Four thin, soft cotton blankets and two thermal-weave blankets. Layering blankets will make it easier to regulate your BT's temperature.

 COMMANDO DAD TOP TIP
Blankets need to be in a position where your BT cannot wriggle under them or pull them over their face. Sleeping bags (once your BT is 8 lb 8 oz/3.8 kg or over) are recommended to prevent this risk.

Nursery furniture

Here are some commonly purchased items for the nursery. Some of these items will need to be preordered at least one month before your BT is due, to allow for shipment, delivery, and/or installation:

★ Comfortable chair (for you to sit in to feed, play with, read to, cuddle, and comfort your BT).
★ Soft lighting (even if it's just a small bedside lamp with a low-wattage bulb). The "big light" used in the wee hours can startle and overstimulate both of you.
★ Blackout blinds or thick curtains.
★ Changing table, if required. I preferred to use a mobile changing station, keeping all my diaper-changing kit mobile and changing my BT on an available stable and safe surface (e.g., the floor or the middle of a bed).

 COMMANDO DAD TOP TIP
You're going to be changing your BT a lot. Wherever you choose to do it, protect your back by making sure you don't need to lean over too much.

BATHING

★ Your BT can be washed with water alone, but if you decide to buy baby bath wash or shampoo, use it sparingly. Buy brands that will not sting if they get in the eyes.
★ Soft flannels and towels.
★ A foam or plastic bath-support that will enable you to use your bathtub for your BT.

 COMMANDO DAD TOP TIP
If you choose to buy a baby bath, it will enable you to bathe your BT wherever is most convenient for you. However, these are large—and will need to be stored when not in use—and it will be used for a relatively short space of time. You may want to consider using a support in the bathtub instead.

BASIC FIRST AID KIT
Core kit

★ Packets of children's acetaminophen and pediatric ibuprofen. If you prefer bottles, use those instead, but always keep backup packets in your first aid kit. Check the label to ensure your trooper meets the weight and age requirements before administering. If your BT was premature, count their age from their due date.

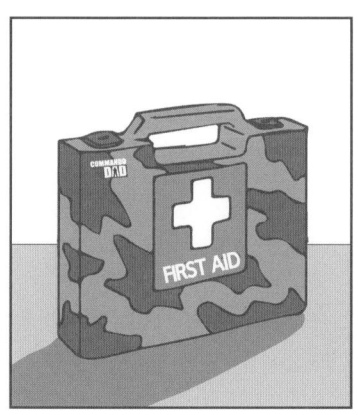

★ Antiseptic cream, also suitable for stings and bites.
★ Antiseptic wipes.
★ Hypoallergenic adhesive bandages.
★ Hypoallergenic tape.
★ Digital ear thermometer.
★ Baby dosing syringe (to administer the medicine).
★ Tweezers.
★ Scissors.

Useful additions (can be bought as and when needed):
★ Cotton balls and cotton swabs.
★ Instant cold pack: when squeezed or shaken, the ingredients react to rapidly cool the pack. It is the equivalent of instant crushed ice.
★ Saline solution and eye bath.
★ Packets of rehydration salts (to replace the salts and minerals lost through diarrhea and vomiting). To be used only on the advice of your doctor.
★ Calamine lotion.

The following items may require you to do a little research in advance to find out what works for you. It is best to do this now, as time will be in short supply when your BT deploys.

BABY CARRIER

Baby carriers are a great solution for transporting very young BTs. Baby carriers hold your BT against your body, leaving your hands free for your many other tasks. Other advantages are:

* ★ Your BT will feel warm and secure.
* ★ The physical closeness may help you bond with each other.
* ★ When your BT is old enough to hold their head unsupported (by about 6 months), some models enable you to turn your BT around so they can face the world.

Ease of use

* ★ Can you fasten and unfasten the clasps easily?

Practicality

* ★ Is it comfortable? As a general rule, the wider the straps, the better.
* ★ Is it comfortable for your BT? Your BT's head and trunk should not be unsupported in any way, but of course their arms and legs can be out of the carrier.
* ★ Is it easy to wash?

Value

* ★ How often do you plan to use the carrier? Is the investment worth it?

STROLLER

A stroller can be a big investment, but if you choose wisely it can last you until your BT is a toddler.

"I wish we'd been told beforehand how important the stroller is. We're on our third one already and Ruby is only 5 months old! We wish we'd spent more time researching and reviewing exactly what we wanted and needed from a stroller/travel system. As first-time parents, we were slightly naive when it came to this."
PAUL HOPE

Ease of use

★ Is it easy to assemble? Can you do it one-handed (you may have your BT in the other hand)?

★ Is it easy to maneuver? Can you maneuver it with one hand?

★ If you are tall, can you adjust the height of the handles to make the stroller easier for you to push?

Practicality

★ If it will be your primary mode of transport, does it have a basket underneath for shopping and supplies?

★ Will you have to collapse and restore it often? How heavy is it? How bulky is it?

★ Will it easily fit in your car's trunk or your house when it is not in use?

★ Is it wider than the average shop door?

Value

★ Does it come with the essential "extras" (sun visor, rain cover, and so on) or do you need to buy these separately?

TRAVEL SYSTEM

Travel systems are a combination of a base with wheels for the car seat and a stroller, and usually include a mobile bed (which effectively converts the stroller into a carriage).

Ease of use

★ Is it easy to disassemble?

★ Is it easy to maneuver?

★ Can you adjust the height of the handles?

Practicality

★ Does it meet all the criteria you would demand of each individual item?

★ Does the car seat fit easily in your car?

Value

★ Would you have bought all the items individually: stroller, car seat (that may need to be replaced within a year), and mobile bed?

★ The carriage is really useful only as a means of transport until your BT can sit up, although it may be possible to use the mobile bed as a first bed for your BT.

★ Do all the parts come as standard or do you need to buy the car seat separately?

 COMMANDO DAD TOP TIP

Strollers are a big investment. Consider secondhand models. Good places to look for secondhand strollers are classified ads in local newspapers, notice boards in newsstands and supermarkets, eBay, Craigslist, and Freecycle. Exercise normal levels of caution if buying secondhand. Always check the safety and roadworthiness of your purchase.

CAR SEAT

A car seat is an essential—and legal—requirement for troop transportation by car. Many hospitals will not allow you to leave with your BT if you do not have one.

Ease of use

★ Can you easily get the seat in and out of your car? Once familiar with your child restraint, fitting should take 30 seconds.

Expect it to take longer at first as you get used to how it works. When buying, ensure that you are shown by trained assistants how to fit the seat correctly to make this job easier and, most important, safe for each journey.

★ Is it heavy, even without your BT in it? If it is, choose a lighter one. Your BT is only going to get heavier, and this could quickly make your car seat impractical.

Practicality

★ Does it fit into your car? Good shops will offer to fit the car seat in your car. Note how they do it. Then practice.

★ Does it provide your child with adequate support while giving them room to grow?

★ Is it safe? Does it conform to federal safety standards?

★ Can you remove the covers and wash them?

Value

★ How long will your BT be able to use the model you are considering?

★ Hand-me-down car seats from friends and relatives are fine, provided they have never been damaged (or been involved in a car accident). Also, check that they conform to the mentioned standards and no parts are missing. If the instructions have been lost, request replacements from the manufacturer to ensure that you are familiar with how it works. If in doubt, seek professional advice.

RECAP AND REFRESH

Chapter 5: Report to the Stores has provided information on:

★ The essentials that you need to buy for your BT. Do not feel you are limited to buying only these items, but be aware that if you buy more than you need, your base camp may end up full of kit that is surplus to requirements. Not a smart Commando Dad move.

★ The basics for a first aid kit.

★ Tips on how to buy essential equipment.

DEPLOYMENT DAY

THE BRIEF

Deployment day has arrived. Today you will need to master the art of being very, very supportive and focused while remaining very, very calm. You need to be guided by your CO, as what she needs from you may change from minute to minute. You are her emotional backup support and as important to her as the medical team. She needs to stay 100% focused on delivering your BT, a huge emotional and physical task. You need to be calm, reassuring, and encouraging in everything you do, and to make her as comfortable—and comforted—as you possibly can.

Gentlemen, if there's one bit of advice I can offer you today it is this: expect the unexpected.

THE OBJECTIVE

By the end of this chapter you will know how you can tell when your CO is in labor and what to do about it, from timing contractions to decamping to the hospital; the stages of labor and the telltale physical signs; and what you can expect in the birthing center. The next chapter covers what happens after the deployment, or birth.

Remember that even if you prepared a birth plan, it may need to change to keep pace with fast-moving events. Certain facilities may not be available, or there may be complications, or your CO may simply change her mind. If the latter is the case, ensure that your CO does not waste any energy on disappointment or, worse, guilt. The best possible outcome in labor is a healthy CO and BT, and whichever way you get there is the right way.

COMMANDO DAD TOP TIP

Be aware that, as first-time parents, you and your CO are going to meet people who want to share their nightmare scenarios of labor—in detail. Where possible, try to focus on your own journey rather than reflecting on theirs. Every birth is different. As a dad to three troopers I can testify that no two births are the same. You need to be realistic about labor and childbirth: it's not going to be all good and it's not going to be all bad, but it's almost certainly going to get ugly. But you will have a medical support team on hand to give your CO all the help she needs.

ADVICE FROM THE FRONT LINE

"There is something about telling other people that you (as a couple) are expecting that seems to compel them to tell you some terrible horror story about their experience of birth/hospitals/labor. You need to try to ignore these people—they mean well, but they're actually causing worry."

NICK BURBIDGE

PREPARATION AND PLANNING
Blood, sweat, and tears

Before you get to the delivery room, you need to prepare yourself for labor, both physically and mentally. To do this, you need to be aware of the following things:

★ Labor is an intense emotional and physical experience for your CO. It is inevitable that you are going to see her in pain, and at times you may feel helpless. Be reassured that she is in safe hands. If you do have questions or concerns about how the labor is going, speak to one of the medical team immediately. You are your CO's mouthpiece—make sure you've discussed the "what ifs" beforehand.

★ Labor can take a long time, and it is easy to lose track of time. Make sure you grab any opportunities you can to eat, drink, and nap. You need to take care of your personal admin so that you can take care of your CO and bring her whatever she needs.

★ There is going to be a lot more blood—and other bodily fluids—than you might imagine.

★ The most effective way to push a baby out is bearing down—the same downward pushing that we use on the toilet. Your BT may not be the first thing to deploy.

★ Your BT is going to be born with a blue tinge and will be sticky and wet with amniotic fluid, blood, and vernix caseosa, a white, waxy substance that protected their skin during pregnancy.

★ The umbilical cord that attached your BT to your CO is a thick, blue-greyish, twisted cord with the consistency of gristle.

★ The placenta, or afterbirth, needs to be delivered after your BT. It will be bloody and purple-gray, with the consistency of raw meat or liver.

★ Nothing can prepare you for the range of emotions you will feel when your BT deploys—it is indescribable.

> ### ADVICE FROM THE FRONT LINE
>
> *"If labor is a long affair, prepare to feel more useless than you've ever felt before."*
> JOHN ALLEN
>
> *"The medical team was excellent . . . they do everything they can to help. My biggest tip would be never to be afraid to ask them for help or advice."*
> PAUL DRAKE

COMMANDO DAD TOP TIP
What happens in the delivery room, stays in the delivery room. I was a commando, but I was never exposed to half of the words my CO threw at me during labor. But I didn't take it personally—and neither should you.

LABOR

Signs that labor may be on the way

As your CO's body prepares for labor, she may notice the following, or she may not. There is no one single set of signs to look out for:

★ Nesting instinct: a desire to clean, tidy, and even move furniture or decorate your base camp.
★ A sudden rush of energy.
★ Increased irritability or mood swings.
★ "Lightening"—when the BT drops down into her pelvis, ready for birth. She may experience this as being able to breathe more easily.

CALL THE DOCTOR

If your CO shows the following signs of labor prior to 37 weeks, get her emergency medical assistance. She may be in premature labor.

How to recognize labor

You and your CO may not immediately recognize that labor has started. Look out for the following:

★ Your CO passes a mucus plug—a brown- or pink-tinged, jelly-like substance that has plugged the cervix shut and kept bacteria and infection out of the uterus while your BT has been developing. This does not necessarily signal the immediate onset of labor, just that the cervix has started to make changes.

For some COs, labor could still be hours, days, or even several weeks away.

★ Contractions. Late in pregnancy, your CO may have experienced practice contractions called Braxton Hicks. Real labor contractions differ from these in the following ways:

» They don't go away. Early contractions may feel like persistent back pain and a crampy period pain.

» Your CO may feel contractions all over, not just at the front.

» Although they may be irregular to start with, they will get stronger, occur at increasingly shorter intervals, last longer, and become more painful.

» The pain will come in a wave, reaching a peak and then tailing off.

★ Your CO's waters may break. The sac of amniotic fluid your BT's been protected and nourished by breaks and the fluid drains out. This is more likely to be a trickle (as your BT's head is now resting in the pelvis and preventing much fluid escaping, almost like a plug), but it can be a gush. There is no rule about when waters break—it may occur much later in labor, and sometimes they are broken in the hospital by the doctor or midwife. You will need to let your midwife know if your CO's waters have broken, though, as without the amniotic fluid, your BT is less protected against infection.

★ Upset stomach/diarrhea. Your CO's body will release prostaglandins in early labor to help contractions and to soften and dilate the cervix. In some instances, these can stimulate her bowels.

How to time the contractions

You will need a way to accurately time seconds: get a watch with a second hand or use the stopwatch on your phone.

★ Time the frequency of contractions from the *beginning* of one to the *beginning* of the next. This will include the actual contraction and the rest time in between.

★ Your midwife will need to know the frequency of contractions to determine whether you need to take your CO to the hospital.

★ If contractions are painful and last 30 seconds or more, your CO is likely to be in labor.

If you have any doubts about whether your CO's labor is starting, call your doctor or midwife for guidance. Ideally, your CO will need to speak to the doctor, not only because she can answer the questions about how she is feeling directly, but also the doctor will be able to discern a lot from the tone of her voice and how she is coping with contractions.

The general rule is:

★ If the contractions are 5 minutes apart, it's time to get your CO to the hospital.
★ If contractions are 2 minutes or less apart, call for medical backup and prepare yourself: you may need to deliver your BT. See "Emergency Deployment" in *Chapter 8: When Things Don't Go as Planned.*

ADVICE FROM THE FRONT LINE

"During labor it is important to admin yourself—take on food and water even if you don't feel like it, and take any opportunities to sleep. You are no use to your CO if you keel over from dehydration or lack of food. The hospital staff will look after your CO's admin; you are responsible for your own."

NEIL WHITE

Decamping to the hospital

Unless either of you is concerned, or your CO feels she cannot cope at home for much longer, staying at home is the best option in the early stages of labor. This is not only because you are likely to be sent home from the hospital (as the early stage of labor can be a long, gradual process), which will be frustrating for both of you, but also because it is easier for your CO to be comfortable at home.

In early labor, where possible, help your CO to:

★ Rest, especially if her labor starts during the night. That's challenging when the most momentous event to ever happen in your lives is imminent, but energy saved now will help later.

★ Focus on something else. Again, challenging. But it may help the time pass a little faster.

★ Take gentle exercise. A gentle walk and stretching—nothing too strenuous—may help the labor progress.

★ Relieve discomfort: your CO may want to move her body instinctively in time with her contractions, or do some of her pregnancy exercises. A warm bath or shower may also help.

★ Drink. Your CO's body is working very hard and needs to be kept hydrated for the job ahead. Frequent urination will also help, as an empty bladder leaves more room for your BT to descend.

★ Eat. If your CO can face food (she may feel sick or have an upset stomach), it will help keep her energy levels up. Light, easily digested food is the best option.

★ Relax. Do anything you can to reduce any stress and anxiety your CO may be experiencing. Be guided by her.

ADVICE FROM THE FRONT LINE

"Be supportive and don't panic. Let the midwives do their job. They are very good at it. Whatever your CO asks of you at the time, do it to the best of your ability. While I was coming out with all the encouragements I could, my wife said I wasn't helping. So I asked, 'What would you like me to do?' She said hold her hand and smile like everything was going to be OK. And that's what I did. She felt better about that and so did I. You are not the best judge when it comes to labor—your CO is—so let them dictate the event."

JAMES FENWICK

Speak to your doctor or midwife beforehand about when your CO will need to head to the hospital. This will depend on a number of factors, including how regular and long her contractions are, and how long it is going to take you to get there. As a rule of thumb, if your CO's contractions have been regular for an hour, are about 5 minutes apart, and last 45–60 seconds, it's time to call the doctor or hospital. She may be in the active phase of the first stage of labor. See "The Stages of Labor" for more details.

ADVICE FROM THE FRONT LINE

"Just before our first BT was due, the weather was turning—it started to snow—but we did not anticipate how much! My partner went into labor and we could not get the car out of the snow and onto the road. Even the ambulance took over 45 minutes to arrive due to snow! So my tip would be to prepare for such weather events before labor. Make sure you call the midwife in time—don't leave it so late that help can't get to you on time."

JACK CARTER

THE STAGES OF LABOR
There are three stages of labor:
Stage 1: Contractions begin and your CO's cervix dilates to 10 cm (4 in). Split into three phases:
- ★ Early (or "latent")
- ★ Active
- ★ Transitional

Stage 2: The pushing stage and birth
Stage 3: Your CO delivers the afterbirth

STAGE 1: Your CO's body prepares for your BT's birth
How long will it last? This is typically the longest stage of labor and lasts from 6–12 hours on average.

What happens? Your CO's contractions open up her cervix, preparing for your BT to be born. It is divided into three phases:

Early labor
Dilation: 0–6 cm.
Contractions: Gradually become regular: 40–60 seconds long and 3–5 minutes apart.
What happens: Your CO's cervix gradually thins out (effaces) and opens (dilates).
This is also known as the latent phase and can sometimes go on for hours and hours, and perhaps even days.

Active labor
Dilation: 6–8 cm.
Contractions: From 40–60 seconds long, up to 5 minutes apart, to 60+ seconds long, 2–3 minutes apart.
What happens:
* Your CO's cervix begins to dilate more rapidly, and contractions are longer, stronger, and closer together.
* You will need to head to the hospital if you haven't already.
* Once at the hospital, help your CO practice her breathing and relaxation techniques to combat her growing discomfort.
* Depending on how your CO is coping with contractions, you may need to be her advocate and communicate her birth plan and pain relief wishes at the hospital, bearing in mind that you both need to go into labor with an open mind and be flexible enough to adapt if the situation requires it.

Transitional labor
Dilation: 8–10 cm (fully dilated).
Contractions: 60–90 seconds long and 2–3 minutes apart.
What happens:
* Your CO may feel shaky and sick as there is a final surge in hormones and adrenaline to give her the energy to push. There's a lot of discharge at this stage—bloody show and other fluids—and she may vomit.

★ As your CO's cervix fully dilates, your BT's head will probably have descended into her pelvis, giving her a feeling of pressure in her rectum.

★ Your CO may have an overwhelming urge to push. You must help your CO understand and follow the doctor or midwife's instructions, as her cervix may not be fully dilated and if so she should not push. If she does, she may tire herself with unproductive pushing. She needs to save energy where she can.

If your CO has had an epidural, she may experience this phase differently. If she wants to actively take part in the next stage, she can ask to have her epidural dose lowered at the end of transition. She should speak to her doctor or midwife in advance about the pros and cons of this approach.

ADVICE FROM
THE FRONT LINE

"I never knew my wife had such a strong grip until her contractions started. Put it this way, I'll never play the piano again! The worst thing was seeing my wife in pain and distress—not something we want to see happen to our CO—but remember she is in safe and professional hands in the hospital environment, and you have to put your faith and trust in them and let them do their job."
CALUM BEATT

STAGE 2: Your CO gives birth

How long will it last? Anything from a few minutes to a few hours.

What happens? This is the pushing stage, when your CO delivers your BT.

★ Your doctor or midwife will confirm that the cervix is fully open and your CO can push. She may have to guide your CO when to push—and when to stop.

- Between pushes, your CO may want to use the breathing techniques she has learned in childbirth classes—help her to remember them.
- As your BT's head emerges or "crowns," your CO may experience an intense stinging or burning sensation; reassure her she is nearly there. It is critical that you help your CO follow the doctor's instructions now, as she may need to stop pushing to avoid a tear in her perineum and help the doctor ease the baby's head out gently, but she may still be experiencing an overwhelming urge to push.
- Your doctor or midwife may need to perform an episiotomy (cut your CO's perineum) to help your BT be delivered.
- Once your BT's head is delivered, your doctor will ensure that the umbilical cord is free.
- Once your BT's head is delivered, it will rotate to the side as their shoulders get in position for delivery.
- Your doctor will guide out the shoulders (the widest part of your BT) one at a time, and the rest of your BT will be born shortly afterward.
- After your new BT gets a quick visual check (APGAR test) and a brisk wipe-down, your CO will be able to hold them in her arms or on her abdomen, depending on the length of the umbilical cord.
- The umbilical cord can be clamped and cut now or, if you and your CO prefer, after the cord has stopped pulsating. This is known as a physiological third stage. The cord can be cut by you or the doctor or midwife depending on your preference. You may need to remind the doctor or midwife if you want to cut the cord.
- Following a brief examination by your doctor or midwife, your BT will be weighed, measured, and given two ID wristbands with your CO's name on them.

 COMMANDO DAD TOP TIP

Cutting the cord: The umbilical cord is a thick, twisted cord with the consistency of gristle. If you intend to cut it, be aware that it won't be a matter of a quick snip. Be reassured that neither your CO nor your BT will feel a thing, no matter how long it takes.

STAGE 3: Your CO delivers the afterbirth

How long will it last? Typically, between 5 and 30 minutes.

What happens? Your CO gives birth to the placenta, your BT's life support system for the past 9 months. It is now referred to as the afterbirth.

★ Your CO will have contractions, although much milder.

★ Your doctor or midwife may massage your CO's abdomen to help encourage the body to deliver the afterbirth, and your CO may need to push. To further help the delivery, your doctor or midwife may offer your CO an injection of a synthetic form of oxytocin—the hormone that naturally makes the uterus contract. There will be more blood as the afterbirth is delivered.

★ Your doctor or midwife will examine the afterbirth to ensure that it's intact. Any fragments that are left inside the uterus will need to be removed to prevent bleeding or infection.

★ If your CO did tear, or had an episiotomy, your doctor or midwife will give her stitches.

★ Your doctor or midwife may rub your CO's abdomen, directly beneath her belly button, to help her uterus contract and keep any bleeding in check. If your CO can breastfeed this will also help her uterus contract.

ADVICE FROM
THE FRONT LINE

"I was not prepared for the mess in the labor room. My wife only lost about 17 oz/500 ml blood, but the place looked like a scene from CSI by the time we were finished. It was a surreal experience having to wipe her blood from my shoes at the end of the evening."
NEIL WHITE

PAIN RELIEF

People have all sorts of ideas and opinions about pain relief during labor and delivery, but there is only one person in the world who can ultimately make the decision: your CO. She needs to discuss pain relief options with her doctor or midwife (with your support) in order to gather the information she needs to make a decision. She needs to explore what's available in advance. Remember: it is your CO's choice to discuss options for pain relief at all stages of her labor, but it may reduce her stress levels if she is fully informed of her options ahead of time.

ADVICE FROM
THE FRONT LINE

"My wife went into the hospital wanting just gas and air, but that quickly changed. Knowing about the different pain relief options helped, as I had to help her make the decisions, particularly when things were moving quickly. I had to tell the midwife that she would take morphine, as she couldn't actually speak at that point."
NEIL WHITE

Here you will find a brief overview of the pain relief available, and the pros and cons to consider. You and your CO will need to speak to your doctor or midwife for more information and to discuss your specific circumstances in order to make an informed decision.

	Type	Method
Natural pain relief can help relax your CO, help to ease her pain, and make contractions more bearable	Heat	A hot water bottle filled with hot (but not boiling) water on the lower back
	Water	A hot (not too hot): • Shower, with the shower head trained on your CO's lower back • Bath
	Breathing	• Your CO can learn some rhythmic breathing techniques for labor, which won't remove the pain, but will make it more manageable.
	Massage	• A massage can help your CO's body release endorphins—a natural "feel good" hormone. But be guided by your CO—she may want to not be touched at all, or only touched gently.
	Position	• If your CO lies on her back it can make her contractions slower and more painful—try to encourage and support her to walk around and use upright positions. She may also find squatting, being on all fours, kneeling on a chair, or using a birthing ball helpful. • She may find lying on her side can help her rest and will not compress any major veins in her body. • Her doctor or midwife will give advice on the best positions for birth.
	TENS machine	• A TENS (transcutaneous electrical nerve stimulation) machine sends off small electrical impulses that encourage your CO's body to produce endorphins, a natural painkiller. It will be attached to your CO via sticky pads on her back.

	Pros	Cons
Epidural Painkilling drugs are passed into the small of your CO's back via a fine tube that is inserted using a long, hollow needle	The most effective form of pain relief, working for the majority of women.	There's a timing issue: • Too soon and it may slow down labor • Too late and it will not have time to take effect before your BT is deployed
	Serious side effects are rare.	Side effects that your CO may experience include a severe headache, numbness, itching, fever, shivering, or a sudden drop in blood pressure (in which case your CO may need a drip).
	Your CO will be monitored closely if she has an epidural, so if she does need help, she will get it quickly.	Your CO is more likely to need help speeding labor up using drugs, as an epidural can slow labor.
		The second stage of labor—pushing—may take longer and your CO may not feel the urge to push. This may mean that your CO needs an assisted birth—forceps or vacuum extraction.
		After delivery, your CO will need to rest until the effects of the anesthetic have passed. She may not be able to feel or move her legs properly for several hours. She may also need a catheter (a tube into her bladder that will drain away her pee) as she may not realize when her bladder is full.

INDUCTION

Your CO may be offered an induction, where labor is started artificially. This may be because she is past 42 weeks pregnant or the medical team feel there may be a risk to your CO or BT's health. Some providers induce after 41 weeks, depending on hospital policy. You can discuss this directly with the doctor or midwife when it is suggested. It is up to your CO whether she has her labor induced or not. If your CO is induced, she is statistically more likely to need an epidural or other pain relief, as induced labor is generally more painful than labor that starts on its own.

ADVICE FROM THE FRONT LINE

"One thing that no one explained to me was what an induction was. My wife was induced and until that point, I thought an induction was a chance for us to go to the ward, meet the nurses, and get comfortable with the surroundings. I got a big shock when I realized that this was not the case."

NEIL WHITE

Induction methods

If you do decide to have labor induced, your CO should first be offered a "membrane sweep" or "cervical sweep" to bring on labor.

Your CO's midwife or doctor will sweep their finger around your CO's cervix to loosen it from the amniotic sac. The separation releases prostaglandins that may kickstart your CO's labor. It shouldn't hurt your CO, but it will be uncomfortable. There may be some bleeding afterward.

If the membrane sweep doesn't work, your CO will be offered an induction using a synthetic form of prostaglandins. She will need to have a tablet, gel, or pessary inserted directly into her vagina. Although she needs to go to the hospital maternity unit for this, depending on the policy of your hospital, you may be allowed to go home and wait for labor to begin. Ask your midwife how long the induction will take to work. Some pessaries are controlled release and may take up to 24 hours to take effect. Others are expected to work within hours, and if they haven't, your doctor or midwife will need to perform an examination to see if your CO requires further prostaglandins. Your doctor or midwife may also employ a cervical foley—a balloon that helps to dilate the cervix.

> ### ADVICE FROM THE FRONT LINE
>
> *"My wife had the dream pregnancy, but had to be induced in the end. That's when it went a bit wrong and all our preparations went flying out the window. As a result, our first month was very rocky. Thankfully our son is 6 months now and is fighting fit. We are loving every minute of parenthood, but there can be a dark side that we all need to acknowledge so things are made easier."*
>
> JAMES WICKHAM

PLANNING AND PREPARATION PREVENT POOR PARENTAL PERFORMANCE

Prior to deployment day, you need to know:

★ Your route to the hospital, at different times of the day, and alternatives.

★ If you don't drive, the number of a very reliable taxi company or a friend or relative who will be on standby.

★ How to accurately time contractions.

★ The layout of your local hospital; where the maternity ward is, and the emergency room, in relation to the parking lot.

★ The best parking spaces and how you are going to pay for parking.

★ Important contact numbers (put them in your phone).

★ If you have pets, someone to look after them. You'll need to have someone on standby to feed and take care of them when you leave for the hospital and in those first few disjointed days.

You need to ensure:

★ Your car always has at least enough gas to get to and from the hospital.

★ You have an "emergency deployment" kit in the car, in case you don't make it to the hospital in time. Read "Emergency Deployment" in *Chapter 8: When Things Don't Go as Planned* for more information about how to cope in this situation. Your kit will need to include:

  » Blankets and towels, clean and sealed in a large plastic bag (to prevent them from getting dirty in your car). You can use the empty plastic bag to store the placenta in until your emergency backup team can get to you.

  » Head lamp (ideally), or normal flashlight, with batteries.

  » Hand sanitizer and/or sterile gloves.

  » Bottles of water, sports drinks, and high-energy snacks for your CO.

You need to take:

★ Change for hospital parking and vending machines.

★ Camera—but be sure to ask if and when you are allowed to take pictures. Some hospitals don't allow pictures in the delivery room, for example.

★ Phone and charger—make sure you have preprogrammed the numbers of all the people you need to inform about the BT's arrival. If you've got a lot of people to tell, you might also want to consider finding a friend or family member whom you can call with the good news, and let them cascade it far and wide. However, you must tell the new grandparents yourself. This is a life-changing moment for them, too.

★ Your CO's hospital bag.

★ Water and high-energy snacks.

FOOTNOTE

Congratulations—your BT is here. Your CO did it—she is amazing. You need to make sure she knows it. Hopefully your planning and preparation paid off and the delivery went as well as it could.

If it didn't, hopefully you were prepared enough to roll with the punches because you were armed with the knowledge that there is no such thing as a textbook delivery. It's worth saying again: the best outcome for deployment day is a healthy CO and BT, and whichever way you get there is the right way.

EMOTION ALERT
Incoming! Gentlemen, expect waves of huge emotions.

RECAP AND REFRESH

Chapter 6: Deployment Day has provided the following information:
* ★ Signs that labor may be on the way
* ★ How to recognize labor
* ★ How to time the contractions
* ★ Decamping to the hospital
* ★ The stages of labor
* ★ Pain relief options
* ★ Induction

* ★ If you want more information about what happens to your CO and BT after the birth, please see *Chapter 7: What Happens Next*.
* ★ For information about emergency deployment (if you need to deliver your BT without professional assistance), cesarean section, or assisted delivery or if your BT needs special care, please see *Chapter 8: When Things Don't Go as Planned*.
* ★ If your CO is expecting twins or multiples, please see the "Multiple Deployments" section in *Chapter 9: Special Ops*.
* ★ If your CO wants to give birth at home or at a birthing center, please see the relevant sections in *Chapter 9: Special Ops*.
* ★ If your CO wants a natural (medication-free) birth, please see the "Natural Childbirth" section in *Chapter 9: Special Ops*.
* ★ If you are a young dad (16–24), please see the "Young Commando Dads" section in *Chapter 9: Special Ops*.

WHAT HAPPENS NEXT

THE BRIEF

The moment that you and your CO have been preparing for—labor and childbirth—is now complete. You both have a new little life to take care of, and it's now time for the next phase of your fatherhood adventure to begin.

THE OBJECTIVE

By the end of this chapter, you will understand what happens from the moment you and your CO are handed your BT to the moment you are able to take them back to base camp.

You can get more information about the subjects covered in this chapter—picking up and holding your BT, changing both disposable and nondisposable diapers, cleaning, feeding and all the associated administration, and burping your BT—in the videos in the "Surviving the first 24 hours" section under *Resources* on the Commando Dad website: www.commandodad.com. You can also find more information on these skills and guidance on baby-proofing your base camp and cleaning your BT's stump (what's left of the umbilical cord) in *Commando Dad: A Basic Training Manual for the First Three Years of Fatherhood*, a book designed to provide you with all the skills you need to be an effective hands-on dad.

HOLDING YOUR BT

Your BT does not have the strength to support their own head, so you must take great care to support it for them.

★ To pick up your BT, you will need to slide your hands under their head and bottom and lift their whole body.

★ If your BT is handed to you, put one hand under their head and another under their body. If the first time you hold your BT is after the birth, be aware that they will be very slippery.

★ To sit with your BT, rest their head in the crook of your arm or hold them against your shoulder, with one hand supporting their head and neck and the other supporting their bottom.

 COMMANDO DAD TOP TIP
Make sure there is nothing in the vicinity that you can trip on. Sounds obvious, but holding your newborn BT can have an almost hypnotic effect upon you, making you oblivious to what's around you.

FEEDING

Health experts agree that breast milk is best for your BT, and you and your CO will both know the benefits of breastfeeding from your childbirth classes. However, just because it is natural doesn't necessarily mean that it comes naturally. It is a skill that often needs to be learned. And remember that your BT is learning it too.

If your CO does intend to breastfeed, ideally the best time to start is just after birth. Your BT is likely to be alert, and their feeding reflexes—rooting and sucking—are strong. Breastfeeding at this point (even if she doesn't intend to breastfeed moving forward) will also help your CO produce the hormone that will help her deliver the placenta and contract her uterus (which may help minimize blood loss). If your CO had an opiate painkiller, your BT may be drowsy, affecting their sucking and rooting reflexes.

Some COs find breastfeeding comes easily. However, if your CO does experience difficulties, she should never, ever feel that she is a failure. It is a basic human instinct to provide food for our young, and it can be frustrating and upsetting if she feels that she is unable to. There are people on hand who can offer help and advice: midwives, lactation consultants, and local support groups. The fact that there are so many people on hand to help shows that lots of women benefit from help and support with breast-feeding. Whatever works for you and your family is the right thing to do.

 COMMANDO DAD TOP TIP
Take the opportunity to attend a breastfeeding class before your BT is born. Do not wait until the first feeding to find out what needs to be done, because at that point, everyone involved is likely to be tired and emotional.

ADVICE FROM THE FRONT LINE

"If your baby is struggling to latch on, or appears to eat very little and often, ask medical staff to check for a tongue-tie that may have been missed."
JOHN ALLEN

Whether or not to breastfeed is a hugely emotional subject, and your CO needs to make the ultimate decision. If she does decide to breastfeed, you will need to offer the following practical support:

★ Make sure she has the equipment she needs: breast pads, nipple cream, clean nursing bras, burp cloths, and a breast pump and bottles if she plans to express.

★ If she plans to express, learn how to clean, sterilize, and make up a bottle of breast milk. Then take the opportunity to feed your BT. If possible, take the night feedings, enabling your CO to get as much unbroken sleep as possible. She needs to recover from the birth.

★ Learn how to store expressed breast milk for later use.

★ Back at base camp, make sure she has a comfortable place to breastfeed.

★ Make sure she eats wholesome food and drinks enough liquids. Breastfeeding can burn an extra 500 calories a day. See *Chapter 3: Fit for Fatherhood* for nutrition tips. You need to look after your CO, so that she can nourish your BT.

★ After your CO has fed your BT, you can burp them. Burping needs to come after every feeding and is important, as it prevents painful, trapped gas.

★ Take the initiative on household chores, which will now also include a lot of laundry. This will allow your CO to focus on breastfeeding without having to worry that she needs to be doing something else.

> ### ADVICE FROM THE FRONT LINE
>
> *"Do not underestimate the role of millions of years of evolution and ignore your instinct. We found that my wife's gut feeling about how the baby wanted to breastfeed was exactly the right thing to do."*
> STEVE COOPER

If she does decide to bottle feed, you will need to offer the following practical support:

★ Make sure she has the equipment she needs: bottles, age-appropriate formula, burp cloths, equipment to effectively clean and sterilize bottles, and a ready supply of clean and sterilized bottles.

- ★ Learn bottle administration—how to clean, sterilize, and make up a bottle of formula.
- ★ Take the opportunity to feed and burp your BT. If possible, take the night feedings, enabling your CO to get as much unbroken sleep as possible.

ADVICE FROM THE FRONT LINE

"We found the whole breastfeeding thing difficult to cope with. My partner wasn't producing enough milk, but the hospital experience is so single-mindedly focused on breastfeeding that it was difficult to get someone to really listen to us. Your partner will really know what is and isn't working; don't be afraid to challenge the dogmatic approach to breastfeeding. She'll also need lots of support because this status quo can result in women feeling like they have somehow failed—which, of course, they haven't!"

NICK BURBIDGE

"The first few months of feeding was like hell for us. The best advice we got and would give to any new parents is 'do what feels right for you' whether it's breast or bottle. When you do that, everything falls into place for a much happier unit."

DANIEL SAXTON

WHEN YOU ARE ASKED TO LEAVE THE HOSPITAL

Be aware that, following birth, your CO and new BT will be transferred onto the maternity ward, and you will need to leave the hospital. This separation may come sooner than any of you are ready for. The best thing you can do is go back to base camp, get some sleep if possible, and ensure that the next day you're waiting outside your CO's ward when visiting hours commence.

> ### ADVICE FROM THE FRONT LINE
>
> *"My wife and newborn BT were taken away from me and I was told to go home. Wow. I did not expect or even know this would happen. I was gutted. However, they were well looked after. My CO and BT needed their rest, and so did I."*
>
> JAMES FENWICK

When it is time for you to leave, you will very probably be sleep deprived and almost certainly buzzing with adrenaline. You may not be operating at your normal mental capacity. Be careful.

> ### ADVICE FROM THE FRONT LINE
>
> *"I got totally lost on my drive home, even though I should have known the way. I was totally exhausted and mentally drained. In effect, we went without sleep for 2 days (labor started one night and our BT was born the following day)."*
>
> SAM WINTERSON

 COMMANDO DAD TOP TIP

Find out in advance your hospital's policies and procedures for allowing new dads to stay after the birth of their BTs, and also visiting times, number of people allowed, and so on. Make sure you have the number for the maternity ward in case you need or want to get in touch.

CHANGING DIAPERS

You may be there for your BT's first dirty diaper, which will appear within the first 24 hours after birth, or you may not. Luckily, there will be plenty of opportunity for you to get hands-on experience in the months and years to come.

ADVICE FROM
THE FRONT LINE

"If, like me, you struggle with the first diaper, don't worry. Within weeks you will be diaper-changing like a pro."
DANIEL SAXTON

There are three stages to your BT's poops, or stools:

★ **Meconium stools:** Meconium forms from materials ingested in the uterus. It will appear in your BT's diaper within the first 24 hours and for the first 2–3 days. It is very sticky and dark green. The best way to describe it is as a tar-like glue.

★ **Transition stools:** This is the stage between meconium and "normal" stools. They are looser and lighter in color.

★ **Milk stools:** Start to appear about day six.
   » Breastfed BTs: Light mustard color, they may have a slightly sweet smell. They can still be loose in texture.
   » Bottle-fed (formula) BTs: Pale yellow or brown, they will have a strong smell and a thicker texture.

Bowel habits in newborns can be slightly irregular, but as long as their stools are soft and pass easily there shouldn't be a problem. Be aware that bottle-fed babies are more prone to constipation, as formula is not as easily digested as breast milk. If you have any questions or concerns, speak to your doctor or midwife or breast-feeding support.

For a video showing how to change a disposable and a non-disposable diaper, go to the "Surviving the first 24 hours" section under *Resources* on the Commando Dad website: www.commandodad.com.

 COMMANDO DAD TOP TIP
What's left of the umbilical cord—henceforth referred to as the stump—will remain attached to your BT for a week or two, before it drops off naturally to reveal their belly button.

In the meantime, you will need to keep the stump dry and clean, to prevent infection. You will need to clean the stump every time you change a diaper. Speak to your doctor or midwife for more advice, or see *Commando Dad: A Basic Training Manual for the First Three Years of Fatherhood.*

BRINGING YOUR CO AND BT BACK TO BASE CAMP

Before you bring your BT back to base camp, you will need to have done the following:

★ Ensured that base camp is safe and baby-proofed. You won't need baby gates right away—actually, they can become an unnecessary hindrance to nocturnal missions in the early days—unless you have a pet, in which case you will need to keep them apart from your BT from day one. However, it is prudent to do the rest of your baby-proofing before you bring your BT home, while you have time to do it. This will include getting covers for unused electric outlets, catches for low cupboards, and protective edges for any sharp corners on furniture (you might also want to consider removing furniture with really sharp edges) and fixtures and fittings. If you have a working fireplace, get a fireplace screen. It will be one less thing to worry about and also give you time to get used to the changes yourself. The catches on the cupboards in particular take some getting used to, so from now on, keep the things you use less often in your low cupboards.

★ Assigned specific areas for necessary equipment, from diapers to strollers. With sleep in short supply over the next few weeks and months, you're going to want to ensure that your base camp is well ordered, with essentials packed neatly away but easy to find.

★ Make sure you are stocked up on diapers, taking care not to buy too many until you know your BT's size.

★ Make sure you have cotton balls or wipes to clean your BT when changing.

You will need to have the following:

* ★ A car seat that conforms to safety standards, if you intend to drive
* ★ A baby carrier, if you intend to walk from the hospital
* ★ A suitable set of clothes to dress your BT in

Clothes for bringing your BT home from the hospital

Your BT will need soft, breathable, and accessible clothes. Cotton is best. Hands, feet, and head will need to be kept covered, as BTs' extremities easily get cold (and a huge amount of body heat can escape through their head). As a general rule, your BT will require one more layer of clothes than you do, unless the weather is very hot.

An ideal suit for bringing a BT back from the hospital would be:

* ★ A bodysuit, a sleepsuit, a hat, socks, and infant mittens—all in cotton.
* ★ If the weather is cold, you may need a baby blanket or two.
* ★ If it's very cold, you may require a snowsuit, but you will need to ensure that if you are using a car seat, your BT can be strapped in securely without causing discomfort.

YOUR CO AFTER BIRTH

Your CO's physical and emotional journey of pregnancy does not end with the birth of your BT. As you will see from the following list, she will now have to go through the process of healing. Depending on whether she needed medical or surgical intervention during labor, be aware that full recovery may take weeks. Even with no intervention, she will be very sore and tender.

Your doctor or midwife can provide you with advice about painkillers your CO can take, based on your personal circumstances, and taking all of the normal precautions. In addition to pain medication, there are practical actions that you can take to help her.

* ★ **Tenderness in the perineum:** This whole area stretched to allow your BT to be delivered, and there may be a great deal of discomfort as the tissues in this area heal and slowly return

to shape. This may be particularly painful if your CO's tissues sustained damage and needed stitches, through either a tear, an episiotomy, or an assisted birth. Your CO may have been given ice packs at the hospital to reduce swelling, and you can use them at home too, although if your CO has stitches ice packs should ideally not be used for longer than 5 minutes at a time, as they will start to reduce blood flow to the area and possibly hamper the recovery. To make sitting down more comfortable for your CO, get her a V-shaped cushion. These are sometimes called back support or orthopedic cushions and are widely available. Do not use a rubber ring, as this will actually increase the pressure—and therefore the discomfort—on the very area that you're attempting to relieve. Encourage your CO to avoid standing for too long as, again, this will increase the pressure in the perineal area.

DOCTOR: STAND BY
Call your medical support team if the pain in your CO's stitches doesn't ease. It may be that the stitches are too tight or she has an infection.

★ **Hemorrhoids (piles):** Your CO may have developed hemorrhoids during pregnancy or while she was pushing during labor. The treatment of them is very similar to that for the perineum already detailed. In addition, your CO should avoid dry toilet paper and instead use moistened wipes, specifically designed to soothe hemorrhoids. She will need to check with her doctor or midwife about using hemorrhoid suppositories. This may not be possible if she has been given stitches during labor.
★ **Constipation:** Your CO may be constipated for a few days after giving birth. This may be because of her nervousness about bowel movements with hemorrhoids, bruising, and stitches to contend with. It may also be a result of hormonal changes, her digestive system slowing down during labor, and/or pain relief that she may have had during delivery. Try to make sure you

provide her with plenty of fluids and high-fiber, whole grain foods to eat.

★ **Afterpains:** Contractions that your CO will feel as her uterus begins to shrink down to its original size. To put this into perspective, the uterus stretched over 9 months, but your CO's body will return it back to shape over as little as 6 weeks. Breastfeeding may also exacerbate this problem, as it encourages her uterus to contract. Typically, the worst of the pain should fade after a few days. In the meantime, a warm hot water bottle or a heating pad can help.

★ **Post-partum bleeding:** Also known as lochia. This is like a heavy period and will last for up to six weeks after she has given birth (although it will get lighter). Make sure she has a plentiful supply of sanitary pads.

DOCTOR: STAND BY
Call your medical support team if your CO's bleeding becomes smelly or gets heavier, as this could indicate an infection.

★ **Excessive sweating:** If your CO is at home, make sure that she has a plentiful supply of clean clothes, preferably cotton. Also change the sheets if she sweats heavily overnight.

★ **Increasing need to pee:** Another way, along with sweating, of your CO's body ridding itself of excessive fluids. If it is very uncomfortable for her to pee, she might find it easier to release it in the bath. This will definitely reduce the sting. If she can't face that, an alternative is to fill a sports bottle full of cool water that she can squeeze onto her perineum while she pees. This will also ensure that the area is kept clean.

★ **Muscle strain and soreness:** Your CO is probably going to ache all over. Soaking in a warm bath can help, as can massage.

★ **Stress incontinence:** Your CO may find that until her pelvic floor regains its tone, she leaks urine. She may find this distressing, but it should be a temporary condition, typically lasting a couple of months at most. When she is feeling stronger, there are pelvic exercises that she can do that will help with this problem.

★ **Headaches:** Hormonal changes can trigger headaches. If you can support your CO to take moments to relax, such as in the bath or taking a nap, this may help reduce her stress and reduce the frequency of headaches.

★ **Breast pain:** Your CO's first breast milk is colostrum, which is so nutrient-rich that she has to produce only relatively small amounts for your BT. However, 3 or 4 days after she has given birth, your CO will start producing regular breast milk, which your BT needs a lot more of. The process of switching between these two types of milk, and her breasts becoming engorged with breast milk, is referred to as her milk "coming in." Her breasts will be heavier and literally fuller. Your CO may find this process uncomfortable or even painful. If she is breastfeeding, this will provide some relief, as will a warm compress (a hot water bottle or a heating pad). If she isn't breastfeeding, it can take up to 10 days for her body to get the message and stop producing milk. In the meantime she can find some relief by wearing a supportive bra. This shouldn't be too tight or it could increase her discomfort and also cause issues with blocked ducts and infection. A cold compress, such as a frozen bag of peas, will also help reduce the discomfort.

DOCTOR: STAND BY

Call your medical support team if your CO has pain in one of her breasts and also has flu-like symptoms (aches and pains and a high temperature), as she may have mastitis. This is painful inflammation of the breast tissue, which can be triggered by an infection.

COMMANDO DAD TOP TIP

Your CO's breasts are factories, not storage containers. In other words, they will regulate demand to meet supply. That is why it may not be a good idea to express milk to relieve engorgement—your CO's breasts will produce more milk and therefore exacerbate the problem. If she is breastfeeding, she may continue to produce more milk than your BT needs (although the excess can be frozen and may become useful if your CO wants to transition to bottle-feeding breast milk to your BT later). If your CO isn't breastfeeding, expressing may delay the process of her body's ceasing to produce milk.

ADVICE FROM THE FRONT LINE

"You will need to do most things for your CO, who will likely be in a bit of pain and discomfort and not particularly mobile. Keeping the home tidy will help keep your mind ordered and reduce stress. Take time to prepare proper nutritionally balanced meals. My wife was pretty sleep deprived when she came back from the hospital, and I remember taking James in his mobile bed into the living room while she slept. I also did all of the housework for the first couple of weeks."

NEIL WHITE

VISITORS

It is to be expected that your friends and family—especially the new grandparents—will want to visit in those first few days and weeks, but make sure you arrange a time that is convenient for you. You and your CO have a BT to look after, and she has just been through the physically draining experience of labor. Your primary concern must be maintaining as calm and relaxed an atmosphere at base camp as possible. You do not need the pressure of entertaining. You'll need to lay some ground rules, which may include visiting hours.

It is inevitable that some people may be a tad annoyed that they are not allowed immediate and continued access, but this will pass. You will thank yourself for it in the wee small hours, when you are administering a feeding having had the benefit of a couple of hours' sleep that might otherwise have been spent entertaining.

ADVICE FROM
THE FRONT LINE

"Don't let people tell you when they are coming round to meet your new BT. Tell them when is convenient for you and your routine. They will expect you to make cups of tea, as if you don't already have enough to do!"

MARK BAKER

That is not to say that visitors are always a bad thing. Visitors can offer practical help: picking up essential supplies on the way over or doing essential base camp admin while they are there: hanging out the wash, doing the dishes, helping to tidy up, cooking a meal, and so on. Your friends and family will want to offer practical help. Let them.

Be aware that visitors may want to give you the benefit of their experience of bringing up troopers. Remember that every BT is different, and use the information that is offered—or not—as you see fit. Anyone who gets annoyed that you are not following their advice is not actually giving you advice; they're giving you orders. You do not have to take them.

ADVICE FROM
THE FRONT LINE

"Do what works for you—every baby is different, and no matter what parents/friends/in-laws tell you or suggest, only you will know what works for you and your BT. It is a steep learning curve, and nothing will prepare you fully, especially the first time round. It is very much a case of trial and error, and as long as BT is safe, well fed, clean, and loved, just do what you feel is right—gut instinct has a large part to play."

CALUM BEATT

COMMANDO DAD TOP TIP

Let people know beforehand your thoughts on visitors in the early weeks. If possible, schedule visits and ensure that people know that there's a set "departure time." Do not feel guilty about turning unexpected visitors away. Your CO and BT are your priorities.

FERTILITY

Be aware that your CO may be very fertile after giving birth. It is possible for her to get pregnant even if she is breastfeeding (even though many believe this limits fertility) and before she gets her first period after giving birth.

ADVICE FROM THE FRONT LINE

"As we left the hospital, our midwife told us that we needed to be careful as a woman is super fertile after giving birth. We both assured her that we were going to take a long rest from baby making. Exactly one year and two weeks later we welcomed our second son—Jude— into the world."

NEIL SINCLAIR

RECAP AND REFRESH

Chapter 7: What Happens Next has provided you with information about:

★ Holding your BT
★ Feeding your BT
★ Changing diapers
★ Bringing your CO and BT back to base camp
★ Your CO after birth
★ Visitors at base camp

WHEN THINGS DON'T GO AS PLANNED

THE BRIEF

We have established in this book that you need to be backup support to your CO. However, in some instances you may both need backup support. Accept help when it is offered and ask for it when it is needed.

THE OBJECTIVE

By the end of this chapter you will have an overview of what to do, and where to ask for help, in a variety of situations. Do not read this to discover all the things that may go wrong—many things may go right. Worry is a negative emotion that achieves nothing. If you have any concerns about your CO's pregnancy, please discuss them now with your medical backup team—your doctor and midwife— as they are the medical experts who are there to help you.

EMERGENCY DEPLOYMENT

An emergency deployment is when your BT arrives unexpectedly quickly, before you have time to get to the hospital or seek medical aid. Statistically, it is not likely your BT will deploy early, especially if this is your CO's first pregnancy. However, statistics aren't going to help you if your BT decides to put in a sudden appearance. Preparation and planning prevent poor parental performance, so review this quick guide to what to do if an emergency deployment occurs.

 COMMANDO DAD TOP TIP
Remain calm and continue to reassure and encourage your CO throughout.

ADVICE FROM THE FRONT LINE

"The main advice I can give is to reassure your CO, try not to panic, and keep a sense of humor about it all . . . it's a natural event, but being on our own was a bit of a surprise."

JON WHEALE, who delivered his BT on a park bench at night

In the event of an emergency deployment, keep calm and follow these steps:

Call for help:
- ★ Call the emergency number in your CO's notes or, if you can't find it, dial 911.
- ★ Give:
  - » Your CO's name, address, and phone number
  - » How many weeks pregnant she is
  - » Any medical condition that your CO or BT may have
- ★ Request immediate medical backup: paramedics and an ambulance.

★ They will stay on the line with you to help you through labor and, perhaps, delivery.

If at base camp:

★ Unlock the doors to allow access for medical backup.
★ If this occurs at night, turn on all the lights to guide the medical backup team to your base camp.
★ Collect items you'll need for the birth:
  » Clean sheets for your CO to give birth on
  » Clean towels and blankets to dry and cover your newborn BT
  » A large bowl, bucket, or plastic bag for the placenta
★ Help your CO strip from the waist down; put a sheet or blanket over her if she wants it.
★ Wash your hands.
★ Ensure that the room you're in is warm and as draft-free as possible to help keep your BT and CO warm after deployment.
★ Ensure that your CO is in as comfortable a position as possible.

If out and about:

★ You need to improvise, adapt, and overcome.
★ When you call for medical backup, make sure they know you are not at base camp, and provide as precise a set of details about your location as possible.
★ Get your CO to the warmest, cleanest place available.
★ If you are in the car, use your emergency deployment kit if you were able to pack one beforehand. See the "Planning and Preparation Prevent Poor Parental Performance" section in *Chapter 6: Deployment Day* for more information.
★ Help your CO strip from the waist down and find her something to cover herself with, if she wants it and there is something available.
★ **Clean your hands—use hand sanitizer or sterile gloves (if you're in the car, check your first aid kit or emergency deployment kit).**
★ Find something as clean as possible that you can use to dry and warm your newborn BT.

★ Ensure that your CO is in as comfortable a position as possible.

Preparing for delivery

★ If contractions are rapid (2 minutes apart or less) and your CO has an urge to push, but the medical backup team has not arrived, encourage her to try panting: 3 quick pants and a long blow can delay your BT's arrival for a few minutes.

★ If you can, encourage your CO to lie on her left side or to get on all fours with her bottom in the air and her head near the floor, as this too may ease the urge to push.

★ If your CO still has an overpowering urge to push—coupled with a feeling that she needs to have a bowel movement, which is actually your BT putting pressure on her rectum as they pass through the birth canal—you need to embrace the situation. Your BT is coming.

★ Whatever position your CO is in, position yourself to catch your BT. If she is on all fours, she needs to bring her bottom nearer the floor, and you'll need to get behind her. If she is in a sitting up position—facing toward you or away from you—gravity will be on your side. Standing up is not advisable, as your BT could emerge very fast and fall.

★ Be aware that there will be a lot of blood and other fluids involved in the next stage.

Delivery

★ When your BT "crowns" (you can see the head appear), encourage your CO to really push—to bear down as if she is on the toilet.

★ Once the head is out, do not pull it.

★ Check that the umbilical cord isn't wrapped around their neck.
  » If it is *loosely* round their neck, gently slip your fingers under the cord and ease it over their head.
  » If it is *tightly* round the neck, leave it, as it could snap and cause complications. Your BT's body will be born with the next contraction and you can remove it then.

★ Your BT's shoulders—the widest part of their body—need to be delivered next, one at a time. Your CO is advised to pant, not push, through this stage to prevent your BT being delivered too quickly and your CO tearing.

★ Your BT's head should gently rotate to one side to prepare for a shoulder to be delivered. If it doesn't, while still supporting your BT's head, gently guide the side of the head toward your CO's back. This should help a shoulder to be delivered with the next contraction.

★ The second shoulder will be delivered next and the rest of your BT will be delivered quickly after that. Be prepared.

★ When your BT is deployed, leave the umbilical cord attached. The medical backup team will be able to see to this when they arrive.

★ Your BT may be born with a blue tinge to their skin—this is normal. They will also be wet with amniotic fluid and blood and coated in a white, waxy substance—vernix caseosa—which protected their skin during pregnancy. They will be slippery—be careful.

★ If your BT has good muscle tone (they're moving and active) and begins to cry, get them dry and warm immediately.

★ If your BT doesn't cry, is blue or gray and floppy, and you can't see their chest moving, then they're not breathing. If you are alone and the baby is not breathing, tactile stimulation should be promptly initiated. Safe forms include slapping or flicking the soles of the BT's feet or rubbing their back. If the BT is still not moving, initiate resuscitation techniques. To learn how to resuscitate a newborn, ask a pediatrician well ahead of your CO's due date.

★ Get skin-on-skin contact with your BT and you or your CO as soon as possible (ensuring that your BT still has a blanket draped over them, especially their head). This will keep your new BT warm and help everyone calm down.

★ As the cord is still attached, your BT may need to rest on your CO's abdomen (as there may not be enough cord to allow them to be laid higher). However, if they can reach to her breasts, put them there to nuzzle, as this will stimulate your CO to produce the hormone that will help her deliver the placenta.

 COMMANDO DAD TOP TIP
If your CO gives birth to your BT outdoors, do not rub off the vernix caseosa, as it can help keep your BT warm. Do pat your BT dry and get them against your CO's skin and under cover ASAP.

ADVICE FROM
THE FRONT LINE

"I now know vernix (newborn cam cream?!) is waterproofing and prevents heat loss, so shouldn't be rubbed off, especially outside in the cold early hours of the morning."
JON WHEALE

Delivering the placenta, or afterbirth

★ The placenta will be delivered after your BT's deployment—typically between 5 and 30 minutes.
★ If medical backup hasn't arrived and your CO feels the urge to push (much milder this time), encourage her to get into an upright position.
★ The placenta will normally be delivered in one or two contractions.
★ It will be bloody, warm, and slippery, with the consistency of raw meat or liver.
★ Gently—as your BT is still attached to the placenta by the umbilical cord—put the placenta in a plastic bag or bucket next to your CO. The medical support team will deal with the umbilical cord and the afterbirth when they arrive.
★ Vigorously rub your CO's abdomen, directly beneath her belly button, as this will help her uterus contract and keep any bleeding in check. If your CO can breastfeed, this will also help her uterus contract.

COMMANDO DAD TOP TIP
Your BT and CO will be exhausted and cold after the birth. You have already ensured that your BT is warm and dry, and you must do the same for your CO. Where possible, remove all wet blankets, sheets, and towels and replace with dry ones. Cover her with a warm blanket (make sure not to overheat your BT).

Breech delivery

Rarely, a baby is born breech—that is, feet or bottom first. If your BT is breech, you will probably know this is the case beforehand, due to ultrasounds, scans, and prenatal checks. If this is the case:

★ Follow the "Call for help" steps, ensuring that the medical backup support team knows your BT is breech.
★ Follow the "Preparing for delivery" steps but, in addition, have your CO get on all fours.
★ During delivery, **do not touch** your BT until their entire body and their head is out, as you may hamper the delivery and cause complications. If you touch their body before they can see you, you may startle them and perhaps activate the "Moro reflex," which will cause them to throw out their arms and gasp (while their head is still in the amniotic fluid).
★ Be prepared to catch your BT.
★ Follow the "Delivering the placenta or afterbirth" steps.

What not to do

There are some things that you *must* never do during an emergency birth:

★ Do not panic. You need to keep clearheaded and help your CO remain as calm and focused as possible.
★ Do not attempt to wipe away any fluid from your CO's vagina, as you may contaminate her birth canal.
★ Do not pull your BT or exert pressure on them. Let them be born naturally.
★ Do not pull on the placenta—let it be delivered naturally.
★ Do not touch a breech BT until their head has been delivered.

★ Do not attempt to tie off or cut the placenta or umbilical cord.

★ Do not give your CO medication.

"After the penultimate contraction, Clementine's head was out . . . I did instinctively pull, and Emma (CO) said, loudly, not to . . . Not panicking, but waiting for the next contraction, is essential."
JON WHEALE

Backup support

When the medical support team arrives, make sure to tell them of any condition that your CO or BT may have, any medication your CO is taking, and any allergies.

Following an emergency deployment, even where there were no complications, it is possible that your CO, and you yourself, may feel traumatized. Do not waste time telling yourself you shouldn't be feeling this way—you are having a perfectly normal response to an experience that you found traumatic. A Commando Dad knows when to ask for and accept help—for both himself and his CO.

Sources of help include:

★ Each other. You can reassure your CO that everything is OK and her feelings are normal, and vice versa.

★ Your doctor or midwife, who may be able to put you in contact with others who have been through the same experience, or know of local places that can provide support.

ASSISTED DELIVERY

Be prepared for the possibility that your CO may need medical help delivering your BT. This can be because:

★ There are concerns that your BT is in distress and needs to be delivered quickly.

* Your BT is in an awkward position and so is not moving through the birth canal as would normally be expected. They may need to be turned.
* Your CO is exhausted and/or is unable to push.

In these instances, a vacuum extractor or forceps can be used. Your doctor or midwife will decide which instrument would be the most appropriate, based on your CO's and BT's situation. Both are safe but may cause additional tissue damage to the perineum. In the event of an assisted delivery:

* Your midwife or doctor will explain the procedure to your CO and seek her verbal permission.
* Your CO will have her bladder emptied via a catheter (a tube inserted directly into her bladder). The catheter may need to remain in after the delivery.
* If your CO hasn't had an epidural, she will need a local anesthetic in her perineum.
* Your midwife or doctor may need to perform an episiotomy (cut your CO's perineum) to help your BT be delivered; this is more likely if forceps are being used.
* Your doctor or midwife will have decided on the most effective instrument:
  » **Vacuum extraction**, which uses suction to attach a cup onto your BT's head. Once attached, they will wait until your CO is having a contraction and advise her to push, while they gently pull to help deliver your BT. This may take more than one contraction.
  » **Forceps**, which are like long, smooth metal salad spoons, curved to fit around a BT's head. They will wait until your CO is having a contraction and advise her to push, while they gently pull to help deliver your BT. This may take more than one contraction.
* When your BT is delivered, they may have bruising, swelling, a slightly elongated head, marks, or small cuts, but these are temporary. Your BT will be checked over by a doctor or nurse specializing in newborns directly after their delivery.

★ Your CO may have to have some aftercare if she has an assisted delivery, as it may increase her risk of developing blood clots. This may include wearing surgical stockings or having daily injections of heparin. Your midwife or doctor will advise you both if this is the case.

Occasionally, if a vacuum extractor has been used but didn't work, the midwife or doctor may then attempt to use forceps. If neither works, and there are concerns about the well-being of your BT or CO, it may be necessary for your CO to be taken for an emergency cesarean section.

CESAREAN SECTION (C-SECTION)
A cesarean is an operation in which a doctor makes a cut in your CO's abdomen and uterus to deliver your BT.

In some circumstances—such as your CO's expecting twins or multiples or your doctor or midwife believing a vaginal delivery might be dangerous for your CO or BT—your CO can choose to have a cesarean. This is called a planned or elective cesarean.

An emergency cesarean is performed when there are complications or difficulties during labor that mean your BT needs to be delivered urgently. It is an operation and will need to take place in an operating room. In the event of an emergency cesarean:

★ Stay calm. This is a stressful, fast-moving situation, and you need to reassure your CO that she is in safe hands. You will be given surgical attire (gown, mask, and so on) to wear.

★ Your midwife or doctor will explain the procedure to your CO and seek her permission. It may not be possible for your CO to sign a consent form, so this may be verbal consent.

★ Your CO will have a drip inserted into a vein in her hand or arm to deliver fluids and medicines. She will also need to have her bladder emptied via a catheter (a tube inserted directly into her bladder). The catheter may need to remain in after the delivery.

★ If your CO has an epidural inserted already, she may have it topped up. If she does not, then she may be given a "spinal"— an injection of drugs directly into the sac of fluid that surrounds her spinal cord. This will have the same painkilling power as an epidural and is very fast-acting (your CO will feel the benefit within minutes).

★ Your CO's abdomen will be cleaned with an antiseptic and a screen will be put up so that she can't see what's being done.

★ Your CO may not be able to feel pain, but she will experience the sensation of deep pulling. She will also be able to hear everything.

★ Your BT will be delivered within 10 minutes, and once they have been checked over, they will be handed to your CO.

★ The surgeon will then remove the placenta and stitch up the wound. On the outer part of the wound they will use stitches or staples that will need to be removed when the wound is fully healed.

★ An uncomplicated cesarean will be completed within an hour.

★ Your CO will need to stay in the hospital for two or three days, and aftercare will be needed. This may include moving around as soon as possible, wearing surgical stockings, or having daily injections of heparin to prevent blood clots. Your midwife will also provide your CO with advice on cleaning her wound to prevent infection, and postpartum exercises.

In a small number of cases, it is necessary for a cesarean to be performed under general anesthesia. In this case, you will not be allowed to stay with her during the delivery.

ADVICE FROM
THE FRONT LINE

"The C-section was rough. I was not allowed in until everything had been set up, and I sat behind the screen as they did their work . . . I felt helpless, but had to stay strong for her. Although she could feel no pain, she felt every tug."
PAUL DRAKE

DOCTOR: STAND BY
Call the medical support team if your CO experiences any of these problems after a cesarean, as they may indicate an infection or blood clot: severe pain, leaking urine, painful or excessive vaginal bleeding, a cough or shortness of breath, swelling or pain in her calf.

IF YOUR BT NEEDS SPECIAL CARE

If your BT is born prematurely, is underweight, suffers from an illness, or experienced complications during birth, then they may need to spend some time in the neonatal intensive care unit (NICU).

These special units are designed to provide your BT with constant, specialized care, and although it can make you feel helpless to see them dependent on machines and medication, rest assured that they are getting the help they need to build their strength and stay well.

In the case of a premature BT, the priority is to provide the care that they otherwise would have received inside your CO's body: help with breathing, feeding, and warmth. This means that your BT may:

★ Have tubes in their nose or mouth to help them breathe, until they can breathe on their own
★ Have wires connected to their body, to monitor their heart and breathing
★ Need to have a feeding tube, which delivers milk straight into their stomach

If your BT is thought to be weak or susceptible to illness, or is already suffering from an infection or ailment, they may be isolated and kept in an incubator.

If your BT requires uncomfortable treatments, such as injections and blood tests, or if they have intense pain because of a condition or an operation, they will receive painkillers in the NICU. Your doctor or midwife will be able to talk you through any side effects. They will also be able to advise you about how much physical contact you can have with your BT. Skin-on-skin contact with your BT and your CO can soothe all of you.

IF YOUR CO DEVELOPS POSTPARTUM DEPRESSION

It is hardly surprising that, after the physical and emotional experience of pregnancy and childbirth, your CO may feel down for a few days afterward. This may manifest as:

* Crying
* Feeling anxious
* Difficulty sleeping

This mild depression is known as "baby blues" and can be caused by:

* Fluctuating hormone levels. After birth, pregnancy hormones bottom out, while others, such as those required to produce milk, rise rapidly. Your CO is on a hormonal roller coaster.
* Extreme tiredness. Your CO will be very tired after labor and then will enter into the sleep-deprived existence that is early parenthood.
* Anxiety caused by having a new BT to look after, or difficulty with mastering skills, such as breastfeeding.

The baby blues may last for a few days and then disappear. During this time, be supportive. Allow your CO to cry, as this is a physical and emotional release. As a Commando Dad, you will be tactful and empathetic.

However, if the blues last longer than a couple of weeks, it may be an indicator of postpartum depression. This is an illness that requires treatment. The good news is that every CO recovers and returns to her "old self." The bad news is that many COs do not recognize the symptoms of postpartum depression or are afraid to admit their negative feelings. This will delay their visiting the doctor and getting the help they need.

Symptoms include, but are not limited to:

* Persistent negative emotions: anxiety, fear, guilt, sadness, or hopelessness

★ Physical manifestations of anxiety: racing heart, sweating, panic attacks
★ Crying and irritability
★ Changes in appetite
★ Taking no pleasure from being with your BT or feeling hostile toward them or you
★ Exhaustion and a lack of motivation to do anything

How you can help:
★ Recognize that this is an illness; she can't help the way she feels. She needs to see a doctor. Go together.
★ Listen to her thoughts and fears and be supportive and sympathetic. Reassure her that she will get better.
★ Try to provide her with time to relax without your BT and also get a break from the household chores. Discuss this beforehand so that she doesn't feel that you have taken over because she is a bad or incapable parent or not coping. Her interpreting your help in this way is a manifestation of her illness.

Further advice and support:
★ Postpartum Support International (PSI) offers support and resources: www.postpartum.net
★ Postpartum Progess: www.postpartumprogress.org

IF YOUR BABY DIES

It is a sad fact that in the United States, stillbirths occur in 1 out of every 160 pregnancies, or about 26,000 stillbirths each year. This does not include the numbers of late miscarriages and babies who are born dead before 20 completed weeks of pregnancy. The death of a baby is a major bereavement, and the stage that the pregnancy had reached does not predict the length or the depth of the grief that the parents experience.

I am so sorry if this has happened to you. Throughout this book, I have focused on you providing backup support to your partner, but if your baby dies before, during, or shortly after birth, you both need help and support. Please do not feel as if you have to cope alone. You don't. This section covers some of the information you will need and suggests other sources of information and support.

Your CO may require surgical or medical support. Your doctor or midwife will be able to provide you with more information, based on your specific set of circumstances. There will be decisions to make. If these are about the care your CO needs, either before, during, or after the birth, legally these decisions are hers. After the birth, decisions about the baby should be made jointly, but don't feel you need to hurry through them. Most decisions can wait.

While she is in the hospital, your CO and you should be cared for in a quiet room where you can't hear other parents and babies and where you can stay together after the birth. You should also be able to spend time with your baby if you want to, and to create mementos such as photographs and hand- and footprints. The staff will suggest what you can do, and it is up to the two of you to decide what you want. Many parents find these physical reminders of their baby invaluable in the weeks, months, and years to come. So even if you are unsure, you might say yes, for example, to having photographs, which can be either stored in your CO's hospital record or given to you in a plain envelope in case you change your mind in the future.

Different states have different reporting requirements for stillbirth, depending on the length of gestation or birth weight. Your doctor or midwife can direct you to staff who will help you with these steps.

Most states require parents to take responsibility for the remains of a stillborn baby or baby who was born alive and then died. The team at the hospital will be able to tell you what needs to be done and what your options are.

If your baby died prior to 20 weeks, it is referred to as a miscarriage. Miscarriages are most common in the early stages of the pregnancy, which is one of the reasons that the initial booking appointment with your prenatal team happens at 8 to 12 weeks. Again, that is not to dismiss your feelings of grief or the impact of the bereavement. There may not be any physical remains of your baby, but you can still mark your loss.

ADVICE FROM THE FRONT LINE

"Our BT was our third attempt at getting pregnant after two miscarriages. I don't think anything can prepare you for the change in emotion after that. We were in bits. My advice for other dads would be: don't be afraid to talk! Whether it's to a good friend or your other half. It's no good bottling it up and being all macho. We have feelings! You have both suffered a loss."

DAVE BOATWRIGHT

There is no right or wrong way to be feeling. The charity mentioned below may be able to help you understand the emotions that you're going through, and how grief manifests itself, physically and emotionally.

More information

There are people out there who have been through the same experience and can listen and offer you support:

★ The Compassionate Friends is a private organization that "provides highly personal comfort, support, and hope to every family experiencing the death of a son or a daughter, a brother or a sister, or a grandchild, and helps others better assist the grieving family." Founded in England, it was established in the United States in 1978, with headquarters in Illinois.

RECAP AND REFRESH

Chapter 8: When Things Don't Go as Planned has provided you with information about:

★ Emergency deployment
★ Assisted delivery
★ Cesarean section
★ Special care your BT may need
★ Postpartum depression: signs and symptoms
★ If your baby dies

By being prepared beforehand about things that *may* not go as planned, you will be forearmed. In the event that the delivery doesn't go as planned or your CO develops postpartum depression, stay calm and support your CO. Help is available. Know when to ask for help—and when to accept it.

In the event that your baby dies during your CO's pregnancy, or shortly after birth, you will both need help and support. As bereaved parents you do not need to cope alone.

SPECIAL OPS

When Your Experience Is Different from the Norm

THE BRIEF

No two parenting missions are the same, but by and large the majority of them do share certain characteristics: they are conducted by parents in a committed relationship, and they give birth to a single BT in a hospital. However, this by no means represents the story for all parents. Some parents are on special ops—that is, their experience is a little special, or different from the norm.

THE OBJECTIVE

By the end of this chapter you will have information to support you and your CO if you plan to go on special ops; that is, if you are expecting multiple deployments, are considering giving birth outside a hospital setting or having a medication-free birth, or are using a surrogate. There's also a section for young dads.

MULTIPLE DEPLOYMENTS

If your CO is expecting more than one BT, a lot of the advice in this book is still relevant to you. She will still need to eat well, take care of herself, and have your full backup support. However, there will be some differences, which are outlined in this section. It is important to remember that, just because twin and multiple pregnancies are considered higher risk, does not mean that your CO will have problems. But she will need to be monitored more closely.

Ultrasound scans

★ Your CO will have more scans than the usual two, usually every 4 weeks until 32 weeks, then every 2 weeks until birth. The frequency of scans will depend on the hospital and clinical need.
★ The first ultrasound scan (8–14 weeks) will confirm whether your CO is expecting twins or multiples. The scan will confirm:
   » Whether your BTs are in the same amniotic sac. If the amniotic sac is shared, they will certainly be identical. If they have separate amniotic sacs, they may still be identical, but it is less likely.
   » Whether your BTs share a placenta. If they do, your medical support team will want to scan your BTs regularly to make sure they're both getting the nutrition they need.
★ The "anatomy scan"—all COs have this around 18–22 weeks— will confirm whether your BTs are developing normally.
★ Additional scans will be available to your CO to check on your BTs' growth and positioning.
★ At 34 weeks, if your CO is expecting twins, the position of the leading baby will be checked to determine the best method for delivery.
★ As with any pregnancy, tests for other rare conditions may be offered where there is a family history.

Routine blood tests

Routine blood tests remain the same as in any pregnancy unless there is a medical problem.

Diagnostic tests

If your CO opts to have screening for Down syndrome, then the nuchal translucency scan measurements will be taken to assess your BTs' chances of having Down syndrome. If a high probability is found, your CO will be offered a diagnostic test that can determine more accurately whether each baby has the syndrome. Discuss these tests with your midwife for an overview of any risks so that you and your CO can make a judgment about what works for you.

Prenatal care

Your CO should receive more than the standard 8 to 10 prenatal appointments so that the progress of your BTs can be monitored very closely, particularly if your BTs were conceived as a result of IVF treatment.

Find out if your local hospital can offer the following:

* Arrangements for prenatal care in multiple pregnancies. This could be a midwife, doctor, or consultant who specializes in multiple births.
* A procedure for multiple births.
* A midwife who specializes in breastfeeding support for twins and multiples.

Delivery

The following are some observations about delivering twins and multiples. Remember, your CO may not be typical, and none of these may apply to you. But forewarned is forearmed:

* Twins and multiples are typically born earlier than single BTs.
* Whether your BTs will be born vaginally or by cesarean section will be determined by how they are positioned or "presenting" in your CO's uterus. Ideally, BTs need to be positioned head down for a vaginal birth.
* Your CO is more likely to be encouraged to have an epidural, not because labor with twins or multiples is more painful, but because it is more likely that your CO will need to have a cesarean.

★ Your CO's delivery will not necessarily be longer or more difficult than a typical delivery.

★ If your BTs are born prematurely or if there are complications, they may need to spend some time in the neonatal intensive care unit (NICU).

★ The NICU can provide the care that your BTs would have received inside your CO's body and help with breathing, feeding, and warmth. Your BTs may:
  » Have tubes in their noses or mouths to help them breathe, until they can breathe on their own
  » Have wires connected to their bodies, to monitor their hearts and breathing
  » Need to have a feeding tube, which delivers formula straight into their stomach
  » Need to spend time in an incubator

COMMANDO DAD TOP TIP
As multiple deployments typically happen early, you're going to need to schedule childbirth classes sooner rather than later. With twins, classes should ideally be completed by the 34th week of pregnancy; for triplets, by the 30th week.

Breastfeeding

Managing twin and multiple feeding can be a challenge. The mechanics are the same, but the logistics are different.

Your CO should be able to produce enough milk, as breastfeeding works on the principle of supply and demand—the more your BTs feed, the more milk will be produced. But your BTs will need to suck effectively to stimulate this production.

As twins and multiples are typically born earlier, they are often small and sleepy, making it more difficult for them to suck effectively. If your CO chooses to breastfeed but comes up against this issue, she may wish to express breast milk. In that case, you will be able to feed your BTs via a feeding tube or bottle.

Backup support

Your CO alone needs to do all the physical work to produce your BTs. A lot of common complaints associated with pregnancy—for example, morning sickness and fatigue—are a result of soaring pregnancy hormones. Your CO has even higher hormone levels than a woman expecting a single BT, so she may experience symptoms more acutely. You may be called upon to offer physical support, such as taking care of your CO and doing extra chores around the house, quite early in the pregnancy.

Your CO may also feel anxious at the thought of delivering your BTs or being able to cope with the reality of everyday life with multiple BTs to care for. Encourage her to share these feelings with you or her medical support team. Both of you need to find out as much as possible about twins and multiple births.

HOME BIRTH

Throughout this book, I have referred to your CO delivering at a hospital. The American Congress of Obstetricians and Gynecologists (ACOG) believe that hospitals and birthing centers are the safest settings for birth. However, she may decide to deliver at home—that is, base camp. If your CO is considered to have a low-risk pregnancy, meaning she has had no complications throughout her pregnancy, is carrying a single BT, and has no serious medical history, then the chances of something going wrong during a home birth are lower.

If you and your CO are considering a home birth, you can discuss it with your doctor or midwife, who can provide guidance and help you make an informed decision based on your personal circumstances and whether support for this type of birth is available in your area.

If you do decide to have a home birth, your doctor or midwife can provide prenatal care tailored to a home birth.

 COMMANDO DAD TOP TIP
Your CO may put a home birth in her birth plan but then change her mind. This will cause no issues, and she is free to

change her mind at any time prior to the late stages of labor. For this reason, it is best for you to know the route to the local hospital, just in case.

Pros

If your CO does decide to deliver at home, there are a number of advantages:

* As your CO is in her home environment, she is likely to be more relaxed than she would be in the hospital.
* It removes the anxiety of knowing the right time to decamp to the hospital for delivery, and you won't have to leave afterward.
* It is easier for you and your CO to control the environment than it is in the hospital:
  » Your CO can move throughout your home and will not be confined to a single birthing suite. She will be checked over only periodically (rather than constantly, as she would be in the hospital).
  » Your CO can eat and drink as she chooses.
  » She has more freedom to choose the room she delivers in (there may be some restrictions depending on your home) and the position.
  » You can dim the lights and create a more "low-key" environment than may be possible in your hospital's birthing suite.
* You are more likely to be assisted in the birth by the midwife with whom your CO has built a relationship over the pregnancy. In the hospital, you will be assisted by the doctor or midwife on duty and, although of course they have equal levels of specialist training as your own doctor or midwife, you might not have met them or be familiar with them. At a home birth, you may choose to have two midwives to assist your CO—one for her and one to look after your BT.

Cons

There are some disadvantages of a home birth that you will need to consider:

★ Your CO's pain relief options will be limited. The epidural is not available in a home setting, for example.

★ If you need emergency assistance, your CO will need to be transferred to the hospital. Cesarean section and forceps deliveries are not available in a home setting, for example.

★ If your newborn BT requires medical attention, they will need to be transferred to the hospital.

★ Any mess associated with childbirth will be in your own home. However, cleaning up afterward will be straightforward: your midwife will bring coverings to protect your home and will clear up the afterbirth.

★ After labor and childbirth, you will both immediately be responsible for looking after your new BT. In the hospital you will have the physical and emotional support and care of the hospital staff. They can provide food, practical advice such as how to change a diaper, and medical assistance and information.

 COMMANDO DAD TOP TIP
If you're using a birthing pool, make sure you have a thermometer and allow enough time to fill it up.

ADVICE FROM
THE FRONT LINE

"My son was born at home, and it was a great experience, really intimate and personal, but also surreal. It was scary while we waited for the midwives to arrive because contractions got closer and my wife said she wanted to push. When the midwives arrived, I wasn't just there comforting and holding my wife's hand, I was actively involved in the birth and getting things ready. After my son was born, I sat and cuddled him on our sofa, which was fantastic. My wife could relax at home—there was no changing on to a ward. The midwives were great and it was really comfortable."

MARC TOPLISS, whose first BT was born in the hospital and his second at base camp

BIRTH AT A BIRTHING CENTER

A birthing center is a small maternity unit based alongside or near a local hospital. It is staffed by midwives and aims to provide a relaxed, home-away-from-home environment for you and your CO. It provides an alternative if your CO is not comfortable with a home birth but would prefer not to give birth in a hospital. If your CO is considered to be low risk, then this could be an option to consider.

You and your CO will need to check if one of these centers is available in your area or within what you consider to be reasonable traveling distance.

Pros

If your CO does decide to deliver in a birthing center, there are a number of advantages:

★ These are specialized units that exist only to support pregnant and laboring women.

★ They are designed to be like a home away from home. Facilities may include a kitchen and lounge area, and TV and music facilities. Check what is available in your local center.

★ Similar to a home birth, it is easier for you and your CO to control the environment than it is in the hospital:

» Your CO will have greater freedom of movement, as she will not be attached to a machine to check your BT. Your BT will be checked routinely via Doppler and palpation.

» Your CO can eat and drink as she chooses.

» It may be possible to dim the lights and create a more low-key environment than may be possible in your hospital's birthing suite.

★ It is possible that you and your CO could meet all the staff at the center prior to her going into labor, meaning that your CO will be assisted by someone she is familiar with.

★ After labor and childbirth, you will have the physical and emotional support and care of the midwives.

★ You may be able to stay at the center with your CO and BT overnight.

★ The birthing center will be well stocked with labor aids, such as birthing pools and birthing balls.

★ The birthing center may also provide supplementary services for your CO while she is pregnant. These could include reflexology, water birth workshops, and prenatal and postpartum classes. Check what is available in your local center.

Cons

There are some disadvantages to your CO's giving birth in a birthing center that you will need to consider:

★ Your CO's pain relief options will be limited. The epidural is not available in a birthing center, for example, but gas and air is.

★ If you need emergency assistance, your CO will need to be transferred to the hospital. Cesarean sections are not available in a birthing center, but forceps may be.

★ If your newborn BT requires medical attention, they will need to be transferred to the hospital.

 COMMANDO DAD TOP TIP
As with a hospital birth, you will need to factor in the time it takes to get to the unit when figuring out when to leave home.

NATURAL CHILDBIRTH

Natural childbirth is a term used to describe a medication-free birth. This can happen in any place that your CO decides to give birth: in a hospital, a birthing center, or at home. However, if your CO gives birth in the hospital, you will need to be her advocate and make sure the staff on duty know her wishes.

Natural childbirth is ultimately your CO's decision, and she will be able to discuss it with her doctor or midwife, who can help her make a judgment based on your individual circumstances.

Pros

If your CO does decide on a natural childbirth, there are a number of advantages:

★ Certain pain medications, such as epidurals, can actually slow down labor. So labor is likely to be quicker without them.

★ Your CO will have more freedom of movement (including trying a number of different positions for birth) than she would if she were medicated.

★ Your CO will remain alert throughout labor and delivery and may be able to take a more active role than would be possible if she were medicated.

★ After birth, your CO will not have to overcome any lingering effects of medication.

★ There is no issue of medication crossing the placenta and affecting your BT.

Cons

There are some disadvantages of your CO's having a natural birth that you will need to consider:

★ Natural methods of managing pain during labor do just that: manage it. They do not eliminate it. It may be very difficult for you to see your CO in pain.

★ Without pain relief, your CO may get very tired. This may impact her ability to push.

★ If complications arise, your CO may need medical intervention. This may lead to feelings of disappointment. You will need to reassure her.

COMMANDO DADS WHO USE A SURROGATE

If you are a Commando Dad who is using a surrogate—either because you and your CO were unable to conceive or because you are part of a gay couple—congratulations on reaching this point. You have negotiated your way through a complex legal process, your relationship has withstood the necessary scrutiny, artificial insemination has been successful, and you have found a suitable surrogate to carry your BT.

Depending on your wishes and the arrangements that you have with your surrogate, you and your partner may be able to be closely involved in the pregnancy and even present at the birth.

As you will be aware, surrogacy laws differ from state to state, and it is essential that you do your research, know the rights and obligations of all parties, and keep abreast of changes to the law.

Your employer may offer some type of leave for the surrogate birth and early days with your BT as part of its benefits package or be willing to discuss special arrangements. Check with your HR department.

YOUNG COMMANDO DADS (AGED 16–24)

Becoming a Commando Dad at a young age can present a specific set of complex issues, but these are not insurmountable. Your age alone does not make you a "bad" dad, any more than every older dad is automatically a "good" one. But you may find that you experience a lack of support, or you are not included by many of the services that exist to support parents.

The good news is that there is help and support out there for you if you need it, but you'll have to take the initiative and seek it out yourself.

Gentlemen, it's probably not going to be easy, but nothing worth doing ever is.

ADVICE FROM
THE FRONT LINE

"Becoming a parent is both exciting and rewarding whatever your age. Inevitably, life changes beyond recognition once the new baby arrives, and being a young dad, I was ready to meet the challenge head on and embrace the change. I am now the father of two boys, and as a stay-at-home dad I've been able to spend more time with them than the average working dad probably would. I've been there at each developmental milestone and have been fascinated to see the way they have grown into little people. Experiencing parenthood at 23, I have had the energy to give my children lots of stimulating play and activities, something I may have lacked as an older dad. Being a dad isn't always easy, but it is the most important job you can ever do."

JAMES HEYWOOD

The following are some typical issues that young dads face. However, you may not be a typical young dad, and these may not necessarily apply to you. Similarly, I may not have touched on issues that you are experiencing.

* **Attitudes:** Unfortunately, for some people "young" is synonymous with "irresponsible." Be aware of their negative perceptions, but do not accept them. Keep calm and show your maturity through your words and actions.

* **Not feeling capable enough to be a dad:** The vast majority of Commando Dads spend time doubting their abilities to be capable dads. We all worry that we might not be able to handle the practicalities of looking after a BT, while at the same time shouldering the awesome responsibility of becoming the most important man in the world to a tiny new life. This is a perfectly understandable reaction to impending fatherhood. However, there is a difference between *thinking* you're not capable and actually *being* incapable. There are prenatal and parenting courses available to teach you the skills you need to take care of your BT; the only thing you cannot physically do is breastfeed.

* **Maintaining relationships:**
  » **With the mother of your BT:** Finding out you're expecting a BT does not necessarily mean that your relationship will end, but evidence would suggest that many young dads do find themselves in this situation. If this is the case for you, recognize that there is a difference between *parenting* and being in a relationship. In other words, although it obviously makes sense to be on friendly terms with the mother of your BT if possible, you do not need to be in a (romantic) relationship with her in order to share the parenting responsibilities of your BT.
  » **With your parents, and the parents of your BT's mother:** Even the most supportive families may be challenged by the news that you are going to become a parent. However, maintaining good relationships with your own family where possible is strongly advised, as they can provide help,

support, and love to you and your BT. If you or your partner are still living at home, then both sets of parents (now grand-parents) are likely to play a major role in providing and caring for your BT.

» **With the professionals who are supporting your BT's mother:** Where possible, engage with doctors and midwives, health visitors, social workers, or the staff of day care centers. They can provide you with information and support that may help you build confidence in your ability to support your BT and their mother.

» **With friends:** You may feel as if you have less in common with your friends now that you are going to be a dad, and it is certainly true that they may not be able to understand your circumstances. However, don't cut all ties with your friends, as this may leave you feeling isolated.

★ **Building new relationships:**
» **With other new dads:** It can be very helpful to meet other young dads who can appreciate your experience firsthand.

» **With professional support services for new dads:** There are specialist information services available for you with staff and volunteers who can appreciate the multiple and complex needs of being a young dad. They can also provide advice on the practical and financial help and support that are available to you, as well as put you in touch with other young dads.

RECAP AND REFRESH

Chapter 9: Special Ops provided you with information about:
★ Multiple deployments: if you and your CO are expecting twins or multiples
★ Home birth
★ Birth at a birthing center
★ Natural childbirth
★ Commando Dads who use a surrogate
★ Young Commando Dads

MISSION DEBRIEF

This is a precious—and short-lived—time. In fewer than 2,000 days the trooper in your arms will be 5 and beginning school; in fewer than 7,000 they will be 18. In order to make every second you spend together count, you need to apply military precision to your parenting: get organized, get the trooper admin squared away, and be hands on from Day 1. Act in a way befitting your Commando Dad status.

You owe it to yourself—and your trooper—to be the best dad you can be. Right now.

GOOD LUCK, GENTLEMEN.

ADVICE FROM THE FRONT LINE

"My advice is what you don't know, you will figure out, and what you think you can't cope with, you will. What parts of it will you enjoy? Not all of them, but the bits that you do, you will remember forever."
JAMES FENWICK

GLOSSARY

Breaking the Code

Medical terminology can sometimes be overwhelming, especially when abbreviated in maternity notes. You need to decrypt the code.

By the end of this chapter you will have a greater understanding of common words, terms, and abbreviations that you may come across over the next 9 months. Abbreviations indicate how this term may appear in maternity notes. If you have any questions or concerns, please discuss them with your doctor or midwife; they are there to help you.

If there's a term not included here, please share it with me—and other dads—on the Commando Dad forums: www.commandodad.com/forum. I will make sure it is added to the *Resources* section of the Commando Dad website and future editions of the book.

A

Active labor: when labor really gets going: your CO's cervix dilates (opens) more rapidly and contractions are closer together.

AFP—Alpha-fetoprotein: a protein found in the blood, measured during prenatal screening.

Afterbirth: the name given to the placenta when your CO delivers it after the birth of your BT. The part of labor when the placenta is delivered is called the third stage of labor.

ALB—Albumin: a protein. Your CO's urine will be tested for albumin, as it can be a sign of preeclampsia (a type of high blood pressure in pregnancy).

Amniocentesis: a prenatal test. A small sample of amniotic fluid is drawn out of your CO's uterus using a long hollow needle. The fluid is then tested for indicators of abnormalities.

Amniotic fluid: the liquid that surrounds and protects your BT and aids in their growth. It is mainly water, but from week 10 onward your BT passes tiny amounts of urine into the fluid. It is the "water" that is released when your CO's waters break.

Anterior position: the preferred position for birth, when your BT is head down with the back of their head positioned slightly toward your CO's tummy. BTs tend to assume this position toward the end of pregnancy.

APGAR score/test: the APGAR test will be carried out 1 minute after your BT is born, and again at 5 minutes, for a quick evaluation of their physical health. Appearance, Pulse, Grimace (response to stimulation), Activity, and Respiration are measured. Your BT will be given a mark out of 10, and a score between 7 and 10 is considered normal. Despite the acronym, the test is named after Dr. Virginia Apgar.

Arrest of descent: when your BT hasn't moved down into the birth canal during active labor, despite contractions and your CO's pushing.

Arrest of dilatation/failure to progress: when your CO's cervix does not dilate to 10 cm (the dilation needed for your BT to be born) despite active labor.

B

Baby blues: in the days following birth, your CO's hormone levels will change dramatically, and this, together with exhaustion and all of the emotions around childbirth, may lead her to feel weepy and/or irritable and "down" after giving birth. These are known as the "baby blues" and last a few days. See "Postpartum depression" (page 81) for symptoms that may require medical support.

Birth canal: your CO's cervix and vagina, through which your BT will pass when they are born.

Birth plan: a plan for how you and your CO would like the birth to go, including pain relief and where your CO would like to give birth.

Bloody show/show: when your CO passes a reddish-brown mucus (also called a mucus plug) that has been sealing and protecting the cervix. A sign that your CO's body is getting ready for labor.

Br—Breech: when your BT is positioned bottom or feet first (rather than head down, or anterior) for birth. This is totally normal, but if your BT doesn't turn to be head first (the preferred position needed for birth), your CO's doctor may decide to turn the baby by hand. This is called external cephalic version (ECV).

Braxton Hicks: practice contractions that your CO may experience throughout pregnancy. They do not dilate (open) the cervix and therefore they are completely safe. When they last for a long time and/or feel intense, they are sometimes called false labor.

C

CEPH—Cephalic: when your BT is positioned head down in the uterus.

Cesarean/C-section: when your BT is delivered not vaginally, but instead through an incision in your CO's abdomen and uterus. This is a surgical procedure, and your CO will be given an epidural to block any pain.

Contraction: the regular tightening and relaxing of the uterine muscle to dilate, or open, the cervix, which is closed during pregnancy. Once the cervix is fully open, your BT can go through the birth canal and be born.

Crowning: when your BT's head remains visible without slipping back as your CO pushes during birth, ready for the final push to deliver your BT.

D

Dilate: to open. Used to describe how wide your CO's cervix has opened. 10 cm is the maximum; at that dilation, your CO is said to be fully dilated.

Doppler: a fetal monitor that amplifies the sound of your BT's heartbeat so that you and your CO can hear it.

Due date: the date your BT is expected to deploy. Pregnancy normally lasts 40 weeks, but babies born beyond 37 weeks are not considered early. Babies can also be late, and if your CO or BT shows signs of distress, the birth could be induced.

E

Early or latent labor: the first part of the first stage of labor, when your CO's cervix dilates from 0–4 cm (her uterus will not be fully dilated until it is 10 cm).

Ectopic pregnancy: when your BT implants and starts to develop outside your CO's uterus, usually in the Fallopian tube.

ECV—External cephalic version: when a doctor turns your BT by hand, in order to get them in the preferred position for birth (head down). Offered if your BT is in a breech position. This can be offered from 36 weeks. It will take place in the hospital, as your CO will need to have medication to make the muscles of her uterus relax, and your BT will need to have their heartbeat monitored throughout.

EDD/EDC: expected date of delivery. See "Due date."

Edema: fluid retention, which causes swelling in your CO's ankles and fingers and elsewhere.

Effacing or effacement: thinning. Used to describe the cervix (neck of the womb) thinning, ready for labor.

Electronic fetal monitor: used during delivery to record your BT's heartbeat and your CO's contractions.

Embryo: your BT in their very early stages of development (less than 10 weeks). After 10 weeks, your BT will be referred to as a fetus.

ENG—Engaged: when your BT has moved into the preferred position for birth, with their head dropping down into your CO's pelvis.

Epidural: an anesthetic injected into the small of your CO's back during labor to make her numb from the waist down.

Episiotomy: a cut made in the perineum (the skin between your CO's vagina and anus) to enable better access to your BT by medical staff. It is needed for assisted birth. Your CO will need to be stitched up after delivery.

F

False labor: unlike true labor, false labor doesn't open your CO's cervix, and the contractions don't grow consistently longer, stronger, or closer together.

Fetus: medical term for your BT before they are born.

FH—Fetal heart: used by your midwife to indicate they have heard your BT's heartbeat. Related terms include:

FHH: fetal heart heard.

FHNH: fetal heart not heard (not the same as there being no heartbeat—just that it wasn't heard).

FMF: fetal movements felt.

FMNF: fetal movements not felt.

Free: refers to how much of your BT's head is "engaged" ("dropped") into your CO's pelvis. Free means that your BT's head is above your CO's pelvis.

Full term: a BT between 37 and 41 weeks.

Fundal height: the distance between the top of your CO's uterus and her pubic bone. Measuring this can help to date how far into pregnancy your CO is, and to assess the growth of your BT.

Fundus: the top of the uterus (womb).

G

GDM—Gestational diabetes: a type of diabetes that some women develop during pregnancy. Diabetes is a condition where there is too much glucose in the blood. Your CO may require medical support.

Gestation: the period during which your BT is growing, measured in weeks; full development is usually 40 weeks.

Gestational hypertension: high blood pressure that develops during pregnancy.

H

HB—Hemoglobin: an indication of iron levels in the blood. If this is too low, it may indicate that your CO has anemia.

HG—Hyperemesis gravidarum: severe form of nausea and vomiting, which can be very serious. It needs specialist treatment, sometimes in the hospital.

Hypertension: high blood pressure.

Hypotension: low blood pressure.

I

Induction: help getting your CO's labor started, also called "being induced." A midwife or doctor can help induce labor using a membrane sweep, a pessary, or a hormone drip.

L

Latching on: when your BT takes your CO's nipple correctly into their mouth to breastfeed.

Latent or early labor: the first part of the first stage of labor, when your CO's cervix dilates from 0–4 cm (her uterus will not be fully dilated until it is 10 cm).

LIE: refers to the position of your BT in the uterus. You may also see Long Lie or LL, all of which mean longitudinal lie (vertical).

Lightening: BT dropping low into your CO's pelvis, ready for birth.

Linea nigra: a brown line of pigmentation that may develop on your CO's abdomen between the belly button and pubic area during pregnancy.

LOA—Left occiput anterior: relates to the position of your BT. LOA means that your BT is positioned head down, with their back against your CO's left side.

Long/longitudinal: refers to the position of your BT (vertical) in the uterus.

LOP—Left occiput posterior: relates to the position of your BT. LOP means that your BT is positioned head down, with their head against the left-hand side of your CO's back.

M

Membrane sweep: when your CO's doctor or midwife uses their finger to "sweep" the neck of your CO's womb to try to separate the membranes from her cervix. This is a method used to kickstart labor.

Monochorionic: where more than one BT shares a placenta.

Multigravida: a woman who has had at least one pregnancy before.

Multipara/multip: a woman who has given birth at least once before.

N

NAD—Nothing abnormal detected: written when the doctor or midwife finds no problems.

Natural or normal birth: an unmedicated birth, without painkillers.

NE, NEng, Not Eng—Not engaged: refers to how much of your BT's head is engaged (dropped) into your CO's pelvis. If your BT's head is not engaged, this means that it is still above your BT's pelvis.

NST—non-stress test: a recording of your BT's heartbeat. Can be used before labor to check heart rate and also during labor to see how your BT is responding to each contraction.

NT scan—Nuchal translucency scan: a screening test to assess the likelihood of your BT having Down syndrome. This is a non-invasive test, done during an ultrasound scan, that measures the fluid under the skin at the back of your BT's neck. Sometimes called a nuchal fold scan.

O

Obl—Oblique: refers to the position of your BT in the uterus. Oblique means that they are positioned diagonally.

P

Palpation: when the midwife or doctor feels your BT by moving their hands over your CO's abdomen.

PGO—Protein, glucose, other: used to record the results of the urine tests your CO has at every prenatal appointment.

PGP—Pregnancy-related pelvic girdle pain/SPD—Symphysis pubis dysfunction: uncomfortable symptoms caused by a misalignment or stiffness of your CO's pelvic joints at either the back or front of her pelvis. It's not harmful for your BT, but can be very painful for your CO. It's common, but severity can vary widely.

Pica: a pregnancy craving for non-food items, such as ice, coffee grounds, and ashes. Please encourage your CO to talk to your midwife or doctor if she is craving non-food items, as some (not ice) are potentially harmful to her and your BT.

PIH—Pregnancy-induced hypertension or gestational hypertension: high blood pressure associated with pregnancy.

Placenta/umbilical cord: your BT's life support system—the organ that connects your CO to your BT and through which they receive nutrients and oxygen. Your CO will deliver the placenta after the birth of your BT; it will then be termed the afterbirth.

Placenta previa—also known as low-lying placenta: when the placenta is in the lower area of the uterus and is covering part or all of the cervix, effectively blocking your BT's exit route. Most likely to result in a cesarean birth.

Placental abruption: when the placenta partially or completely separates from the uterus (womb) before your BT is delivered.

Posterior position: refers to the position of your BT in the uterus. The back of your BT's head is toward your CO's back.

Postpartum: after the birth.

Postpartum depression: depression that occurs after the deployment of your BT. While it is common to feel a little down after birth—sometimes referred to as "baby blues"—if this is prolonged or chronic, speak to your medical support team.

Preeclampsia: a potentially serious condition characterized by the onset of high blood pressure (where blood pressure was previously normal) and protein in the urine.

Prenatal: before the birth of your BT. Sometimes called antenatal or antepartum.

Prenatal depression: a rarer condition than postpartum depression, but equally debilitating. Seek support from your medical backup team.

Prenatal steroids: steroids given to help your BT's lungs and other organs mature more rapidly when it is expected they will be delivered preterm (before 36 weeks).

Prepartum: before the birth of your BT. Sometimes called prenatal or antenatal.

Presentation: the position of your BT—the part of their body "presenting" will be born first.

Preterm/premature: before the full term of the pregnancy is complete; generally earlier than 37 weeks.

Primigravida: a woman pregnant for the first time.

Primipara (Prim/Primip): a woman giving birth for the first time.

Prot—Protein: refers to your CO's urine test and whether protein has been found. Plus signs (+) are used to indicate the levels of protein found, with 3 being the highest level. Nil means no protein was found, and Tr means a trace of protein has been found.

Proteinuria: protein in your CO's urine.

Q

Quickening: the first movements of your BT that your CO can feel. May feel like a fluttering or a bubbling inside.

R

ROA—Right occiput anterior: refers to the position of your BT in the uterus. ROA means that your BT is positioned head down, with their back against your CO's right side.

Rooting/rooting reflex: your BT will instinctively search for your CO's breast to feed; the rooting reflex consists of head turning and sucking movements.

ROP—Right occiput posterior: refers to the position of your BT in the uterus. In this case, it means your BT is positioned head down, with their head against the right-hand side of your CO's back.

S

Show/bloody show: while your CO is pregnant, the cervix is sealed shut with a mucus plug. Just before labor starts, or in early labor, your CO's cervix will open and the plug will come out. Your CO may see this "show" as a pink (or brown) jelly-like substance. Some COs do not know they have lost the plug and do not have a show.

Sonogram/ultrasound: a procedure that uses high-frequency sound waves to create an image of your unborn BT. Can help to date how far into pregnancy your CO is and to assess the growth of your BT.

SPD—Symphysis pubis dysfunction/PGP—pregnancy-related pelvic girdle pain: uncomfortable symptoms caused by a misalignment or stiffness of your CO's pelvic joints at either the back or front of her pelvis. It's not harmful for your BT, but can be very painful for your CO. It's common, but severity can vary widely.

SROM—Spontaneous rupture of membranes: when your CO's waters break naturally when she's full term and in labor.

Stages of labor: labor is divided into three stages. The first stage leads up to the actual birth and has three phases: early labor, active labor, and the transitional phase. The second stage is when your CO delivers your BT. The third stage is when your CO delivers the placenta (your BT's life support system for the past nine months), called the afterbirth after it's delivered.

T

Term: the amount of time it takes a BT to fully develop: 37–42 weeks.

Tr—Transverse: refers to the position of your BT in the uterus. Transverse means that they are positioned across your CO's body, and if your BT cannot be turned, a cesarean will be required.

Trimester: a word meaning "three months." Pregnancy is divided into three trimesters—three periods of three months—the first, second, and third trimesters.

Triple test: a blood test that may indicate the probability of chromosomal abnormalities. It will not determine whether your BT will definitely be affected, but will help you and your CO decide if you wish to have a diagnostic (invasive) test to be certain. It measures three substances in your CO's blood—alpha-fetoprotein (AFP), unconjugated estriol (UE), and human chorionic gonadotropin (hCG)—hence the name "triple test."

U

Ultrasound scan/sonogram: a procedure that uses high-frequency sound waves to create an image of your unborn BT. It can help to date how far into pregnancy your CO is and to assess the growth of your BT.

Umbilical cord/placenta: your BT's life support system—the organ that connects your CO to your BT and through which they receive nutrients and oxygen. Your CO will deliver the placenta after the birth of your BT; it will then be termed the afterbirth.

Uterus: a medical term for the womb, where your BT grows.

V

Vacuum extractor: a medical device that may be used to help deliver your BT. A suction cup is put onto your BT's head to help guide them out.

VE: vaginal examination.

Vernix caseosa: a white, waxy substance that develops around your BT to protect their skin from amniotic fluid. It is absorbed into your BT's skin shortly after birth.

VX—Vertex: the crown (top) of your BT's head.

W

Waters breaking: term for when the bag of fluid that has surrounded and protected your BT—the amniotic sac—breaks, and the fluid leaks out. It can be either a trickle or a gush. If your CO's waters break before labor starts, phone your doctor or midwife. Without amniotic fluid, your BT is less protected from infection.

Z

Zygote: a fertilized egg—the start of your BT.

Index

A

Abdominal pain, 77
Acetaminophen, 82, 92
Acne, 23
AFP (alpha-fetoprotein), 46
Afterbirth, 101, 110, 140
Afterpains, 129
Alcohol, 41, 58–60
Amniocentesis, 47
Amniotic fluid, 103
Anatomy scan, 38, 47–48
Ankles, swollen, 30, 76, 78
APGAR test, 109
Appetite, increased, 25

B

Baby. *See also* Changing;
  Feeding
  bowel habits of, 125
  clothing for, 86–87, 127
  death of, 148–50
  development of, 18, 19–20,
  22–23, 24, 26, 27–28, 29, 31,
  33
  finding out sex of, 47–48
  heartbeat of, 47
  holding, 120
  premature, 146–47
  seeing, for first time, 38, 44
  skull of, 31

Baby blues, 49, 78, 147
Baby carriers, 93, 127
Baby monitors, 90
Baby-proofing, 126
Back pain, 32, 34, 77
Balance, sense of, 28, 32
Bassinets, 90
Bathing, 91
Birth. *See also* Labor; Multiple
  births
  assisted, 142–44
  at birthing center, 13, 160–61
  breech, 141
  cesarean, 144–46
  emergency, 136–42
  at home, 13, 137, 157–59
  mother's healing after,
  127–30
  natural childbirth, 161–62
  preparing for, 100–101,
  115–17, 138
  process of, 108–9, 138–40
  still-, 148–49
Birthing centers, 13, 160–61
Birthing pools, 159
Birth plan, 51–52, 99
Blankets, 86, 90
Bleeding
  postpartum, 129
  vaginal, 76, 77

Blood clots, 77

Blood pressure
high, 40, 42, 59, 79
low, 21

BMI (body mass index), 41–42

Bottle feeding
equipment for, 89
providing support for, 122–23

Braxton Hicks contractions, 32, 78, 103

Breastfeeding
benefits of, 120
classes, 121
difficulties with, 121
equipment for, 89, 121
expressing milk, 130–31
information about, 43
providing support for, 121–22
starting, 120–21
of twins and multiples, 156

Breasts
engorged, 130–31
larger, 20
leaking, 25, 34
painful, 130
sensitive, 21

Breath, shortness of, 30

Breech delivery, 141

Burping, 122, 123

C

Carpal tunnel syndrome, 28

Car seats, 94, 95–96, 127

Cervical sweep, 114

Cesarean section, 144–46

Changing
diapers, 87, 124–25
kit, 87
table, 91

Childbirth classes, 43, 52–55

Chills, 77

Cholestasis, 29, 81

Clothing, 86–87, 127

Colostrum, 25, 34, 130

Compassionate Friends, 150

Constipation, 22, 128–29

Contractions
afterpains, 129
Braxton Hicks, 32, 78, 103
frequency of, 103–4
real, 78–79, 103

Cramps, 30, 77

Cravings, 21, 65–66

Cribs, 90

C-section, 144–46

CV (chorionic villus) sampling, 46

D

Dating scan, 38, 41, 44

Death, of baby, 148–50

Delivery. *See* Birth

Depression, 49, 78, 81, 147–48

Diabetes, gestational, 41, 42, 81

Diagnostic tests, 46–47, 155

Diapers, 87, 124–25

Diarrhea, 69, 80, 92, 103

Dizziness, 19, 21, 77

Down syndrome, 42, 45, 155

Dry eye syndrome, 28

E

Ectopic pregnancy, 76, 77, 80
Emotions, dealing with, 12, 16
Energy, increased, 25
Epidurals, 108, 113, 114, 144, 155, 162
Episiotomy, 109, 110, 128, 143
Equipment
    baby carrier, 93, 127
    for bathing, 91
    car seat, 94, 95–96, 127
    changing kit, 87
    for feeding, 89–90, 121
    first aid kit, 92
    kitbag, 87–88
    for sleeping, 90
    stroller, 93–94, 95
    travel system, 94–95
Exercise, 60–64, 72
Eyes, dry, 28

F

Fainting, 19
Family history, 41
Fatherhood
    preparing for, 10, 57–73
    young dads and, 163–65
Fatigue, 21
Fear, 10, 12
Feeding. *See also* Bottle feeding; Breastfeeding
    equipment for, 89–90
    providing support for, 120–23
Feet, swollen, 30, 76, 78
Fertility, after birth, 133

Fetal alcohol syndrome (FAS), 59
Fever, 77
Fingers
    achy, 30
    swollen, 30
First aid kit, 92
First trimester, 17, 18–24
Fish, 67, 69–70
Fitness, 60–64, 72
Fontanelle, 31
Food
    to avoid, 68–70
    cravings, 21, 65–66
    eating for two, 65
    groups, recommended, 66–67
    importance of, 64–65
    preparing, 70, 71–72
    processed, 68
Forceps, 143, 144
Formula feeding. *See* Bottle feeding
4D scans, 51
Frustration, 34

G

Golden rules, 13
Group B strep, 49

H

Hair growth, 20, 23
Hands
    achy, 30
    swollen, 30, 78
hCG (human chorionic gonadotropin), 46

Headaches, 30, 76, 77, 130
Heartbeat, fetal, 47
Heartburn, 22, 25
Hemorrhoids, 30, 128
Herbal remedies, 82
HIV, 42, 49
Home births, 13, 137, 157–59
Hospital
    going to, 104–6
    leaving, 123–24, 126–27
Hyperemesis gravidarum, 19,
    78, 81

I
Ibuprofen, 92
Incontinence, 129–30
Induction, 51, 114–15
Itching, 28, 29, 78

K
Kitbag, 87–88

L
Labor. *See also* Birth;
    Contractions
    false, 32
    horror stories about, 100
    inducing, 51, 114–15
    pain relief during, 111–13
    premature, 76, 77, 80, 102
    preparing for, 100–101,
    115–17
    signs of, 102–3
    stages of, 106–10
Lanugo, 28, 33
Laundry, 87

Leaking fluid, 77
Leg cramps, 30, 77
Lifestyle, adopting healthy, 20,
    35, 41, 57–73
Lightening, 34, 102
Linea nigra, 23
Listeriosis, 68–69
Lochia, 129

M
Mastitis, 130
Meconium, 125
Medications, 82
Membrane sweep, 114
Mercury, 69–70
Midwives, 39–40, 158
Miscarriages, 76, 149–50
Mood swings, 16, 21, 78
Morning sickness, 19, 76
Moro reflex, 141
Mucus plug, 77, 102
Multiple births, 35, 38, 44, 53,
    154–57
Muscle strain and soreness, 129

N
Natural childbirth, 161–62
Nausea, 78, 79, 81. *See also*
    Morning sickness; Vomiting
Neonatal intensive care unit
    (NICU), 146–47, 156
Nose
    -bleeds, 25
    runny or stuffy, 21
Nuchal translucency scan,
    45–46, 155

Nursery furniture, 91
Nutrition, 64–72

O
Obstetric cholestasis, 29, 81
Oxytocin, 110

P
Pain
    abdominal, 77
    back, 32, 34, 77
    breast, 130
    pelvic, 32, 77
Pain relief
    after birth, 127
    during labor, 111–13
    natural methods of, 162
Pelvic pain, 32, 77
Perineum, tenderness in,
    127–28
Pica, 66
Placenta
    delivery of, 101, 110, 140
    previa, 76, 80
Placental abruption, 76, 79
Planning, importance of, 13,
    115–17
Postpartum bleeding, 129
Postpartum depression, 49, 78,
    81, 147–48
Preeclampsia, 30, 42, 77, 78, 79
Pregnancy. *See also* Trimesters
    ectopic, 76, 77, 80
    telling people about, 44–45,
    48
    tests, 40

Premature babies, 146–47
Premature labor, 76, 77, 80, 102
Prenatal care, 37–51, 155
Progesterone, 21, 22, 25

Q
Quickening, 25

R
Rhesus positive or negative,
    42, 49

S
Second trimester, 17, 24–29
Skin
    itchy, 28, 29
    oily, 23
Sleeping
    equipment for, 90
    problems, 24
Smell, heightened sense of, 21
Smoking, 41, 58
Spina bifida, 42
Spotting, 76, 79
Sterilization equipment, 89–90
Stillbirths, 148–49
Strep, 49
Stress incontinence, 129–30
Stretch marks, 28
Strollers, 93–94, 95
Supplements, 70–71
Surrogates, 162–63
Sweating, 27, 129
Swelling, 30, 78
Symphysis pubis dysfunction,
    32

T

TENS machine, 112
Third trimester, 17, 29–34
3D scans, 51
Thrombosis, deep vein, 77
Travel systems, 94–95
Trimesters
  first, 17, 18–24
  second, 17, 24–29
  start and end dates of, 17
  third, 17, 29–34
Triple test, 45, 46
Twins, 35, 38, 44, 53, 154–57

U

UE (unconjugated estriol), 46
Ultrasound scans, 23, 24, 44,
  141, 154
Umbilical cord
  appearance of, 101
  around neck, 138
  cutting, 109–10
  stump, cleaning, 125–26
Urination
  after birth, 129–30
  incontinence, 129–30
  during pregnancy, 21, 22, 25,
  30, 34
  problems with, 78

V

Vacuum extraction, 143, 144
Vaginal bleeding, 76, 77
Vaginal discharge, 28, 29, 77
Varicose veins, 30
Vernix caseosa, 26, 101, 140
Vision problems, 77
Visitors, 131–33
Vitamins
  A, 69, 71
  C, 70
  D, 70
  K, 49
  supplements, 70–71
Vomiting, 19, 77, 78. *See also*
  Morning sickness

W

Waters breaking, 77, 103
Weight
  gain, 17–18
  loss, 19

Y

Young dads, 163–65

Acknowledgments

Thanks to the following people for their help in reviewing and approving content:

★ Kate Bedding, research and education consultant, LSA auditor, NCT prenatal teacher, Preparation for Birth & Beyond teacher, and postnatal facilitator and public governor of Liverpool Women's NHS Foundation Trust Hospital, for reviewing the whole manuscript and being a constant source of support

★ Mark Clement-Jones, consultant obstetrician, Liverpool Women's NHS Foundation Trust Hospital, for reviewing the whole manuscript and making positive suggestions

★ Andrea Smith, midwife, Samuel Johnson Midwifery led unit, Lichfield, for reviewing *Chapter 1: New Recruits*, *Chapter 2: Actions on Appointments*, *Chapter 7: What Happens Next*, and *Chapter 8: When Things Don't Go as Planned* brilliantly, and on short notice

★ The British Red Cross Society, which has approved the first aid information in the "Emergency Deployment" section of *Chapter 8: When Things Don't Go as Planned*

★ Alix Henley and Judith Schott from Sands, the stillbirth and neonatal death charity, who helped with the section "If Your Baby Dies" in *Chapter 8: When Things Don't Go as Planned*

★ Dr. Gary Brickley, senior lecturer in sports and exercise science at the University of Brighton, chartered scientist, British Association of Sport and Exercise accredited scientist, and international coach, for his help with *Chapter 3: Fit for Fatherhood*

★ Ian North, development manager, Dads4Dads, for not only reviewing the young dads section, but also helping me find dads who were willing to share their stories

★ Stacey Wills, from the Twins and Multiple Births Association (TAMBA), for reviewing the sections on twins and multiples

Honor Roll

Thanks to the following folks, who responded to my "call to arms" for help with this book. They shared their experiences; offered advice, support, guidance, and tips; and even provided some brilliant quotes.

Adam Baker
Andrew Brooker
Andy Long
Andy McKevitt
Calum Beatt
Chris Simpson
Christopher Jones
Dan Fuller
Daniel Saxton
Dave Boatwright
David Topping
Devlin Waddell
Devon Starmer
Ed Rankin
Edward Starmer
Grant Mills
Hywel Davies
Ian North
Jack Carter
James Fenwick
James Gibbs
James Heywood
James Waddell
James Wickham
Jamie Williams
Jennifer Gray
John Allen
Jon Watkins
Jon Wheale

Kevin S
Lee Parker
Lee Richardson
Leigh Greenwood
Liam D
Marc Topliss
Mark Baker
Mark Yates
Martin Scott
Matt Richards
Matthew Walker-Rowe
Neil Mawson
Neil White
Nick Burbidge
Nick Dawson
Paul Drake
Paul Hope
Philip Sowerby
Rich Brown
Rob Falls
Ron Murray
Sam Winterson
Stephen Ellis
Steve Cooper
Stuart Cooper
Tony Barnett
Tony Ewart
William Adams